The woman moaned. C. J. . . . lived for these moments when she could drive some woman to the point of no return. To the point to where for a few precious moments, some woman needed her more than anything else did on earth . . . C. J. moved her toward a littered desk a few feet away. Once there, C. J. picked the woman up and laid her across it. She spread the woman's legs and stood between them, leaning over and kissing her deeply . . . C. J.'s heart soared as the woman came with a series of loud groans that C. J. was certain anyone in the store would be able to hear.

LOOKING FOR NAIAD?

Buy our books at
www.naiadpress.com

or call our toll-free number
1-800-533-1973

or by fax (24 hours a day)
1-850-539-9731

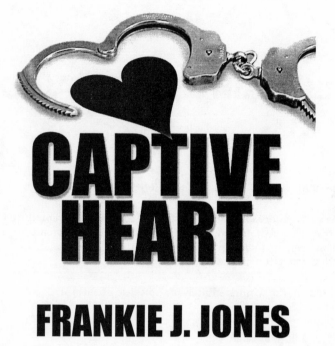

CAPTIVE HEART

FRANKIE J. JONES

THE NAIAD PRESS, INC.
1999

Printed in the United States of America on acid-free paper
First Edition

Editor: Lila Empson
Cover designer: Bonnie Liss (Phoenix Graphics)
Typesetter: Sandi Stancil

Library of Congress Cataloging-in-Publication Data

Jones, Frankie J., 1953 –
  Captive heart / by Frankie J. Jones.
     p.   cm.
  ISBN 1-56280-258-5 (alk. paper)
  I. Title.
PS3560.04825C36 1999
813'.54—dc21

99-18393
CIP

For Peggy

Acknowledgments

I would like to thank Peggy J. Herring, for being my first and second reader, and Martha Cabrera, for reading the manuscript and making sure Peggy was being impartial.

About the Author

Frankie J. Jones is the author of *Rhythm Tide* and *Whispers in the Wind*. She enjoys metal detecting, long walks, conversations without timers, and lazy Sundays.

CHAPTER ONE

C. J. wove her forest green Jaguar V12 across lanes and around cars, heedless of the blaring horns. The heavy traffic closed around her, forcing her to reduce the speed of the powerful engine to sixty-five miles per hour. She was trapped in the right lane. Glancing at her watch, she groaned. An opening appeared and, accompanied by the blaring protest of yet another irate driver, she whipped the car into the center lane.

This whole fiasco had started when the board meeting ran until after six. *Why do I have to attend those damn things anyway?* she wondered. After the meeting she raced home to change clothes only to find that her favorite pants were not back from the cleaners. Another valuable ten minutes were wasted screaming at the housekeeper, who had failed to pick up the dry cleaning. She was over an hour late for her date with Anne.

C. J. already knew how the evening would progress. Anne would pull the cold silent treatment, and C. J. would spend the night trying to find ways to make it up to her. Tomorrow she would send Anne flowers and maybe jewelry, perhaps those earrings at Rosenbloom's she had been hinting for, and eventually Anne would forgive her. But tonight C. J. would be sent home.

The announcer on the radio began to drone on about the police officer who had been killed a few days earlier. The officer had stopped a car for a routine traffic violation. The driver had been a wanted fugitive and had shot the officer as he walked up to the car. Irritated with the interruption to the music, C. J. popped in a CD. Instead of the rock and roll she had anticipated, a loud grinding noise filled the speakers just before the CD ejected. Nothing was going right. C. J. turned her attention to the CD player, trying to convince the disc to stay in.

"Is it too much to ask for to want to hear music rather than the news? There's never anything good to hear anyway. Who needs to hear about other people's depressing lives?" Her ranting was cut short as a movement in front of her caught her attention.

"Damn!" She grasped the steering wheel and

slammed on the brakes as a small, slow-moving truck pulled in front of her. She blared her horn and made a couple of rude hand gestures at the old man driving. He continued at his snail's pace and studiously ignored her.

Having given up on the CD, she grabbed her mobile phone and punched in Anne's number, knowing there would be no answer. The answering service had been turned off. Anne was making her annoyance known by refusing to answer the phone. She did this every time C. J. was late. When C. J. finally arrived, Anne would harp for hours about C. J. not calling to let her know she was going to be late.

A break in traffic appeared in the left lane, and an eighteen-wheeler pulled from behind C. J. and barreled along beside her. "Not this time buddy," she growled and pressed the accelerator harder. The Jag shot forward, and C. J. slid smoothly in front of the truck. She breathed a sigh of relief at the open road in front of her. Caught up in the exhilaration of pushing the car's powerful engine, it took her a minute to comprehend the flashing lights in her rearview mirror.

A string of oaths and a considerable amount of steering-wheel pounding accompanied her exit to the shoulder of the road. The semi roared by with a loud mocking blare of his horn. C. J. shot him the finger before turning her attention to the flashing lights behind her. She removed her sunglasses as she glimpsed the tall, thin form of the police officer emerging from the vehicle. She could see only the long, blue gray-clad legs moving slowly toward her.

"That's it. The last straw," she fumed, grabbing

her driver's license from the visor. "I'll show this asshole who he's dealing with and Anne can damn well understand. I'm not kissing another ass today!"

Flinging the seat belt off she jumped out of the car and found herself staring down the barrel of a very large pistol.

"What the hell?" she squeaked, throwing her hands up, unable to take her eyes off the weapon.

"Against the car!"

"Wait a minute."

"I said against the car. *Now!*"

C. J. quickly complied. The cop briskly patted her down. Anger replaced her fright. "If you're through with your cheap thrills, would you like to explain what you think you're doing?"

"You can turn around," the officer replied, replacing the weapon in its holster and stepping away. "As for explaining, why don't you start by telling me where the fire is? And in the future, I suggest you stay in your vehicle when a patrol car pulls you over. An officer was killed last week, and we tend to get a little nervous when people come flying out of their vehicles like you did."

C. J. turned to retort but was brought up short by the sight of the tall woman standing before her. The visor on her cap and the reflective shades hid much of the thin, deeply tanned face that was framed by short, curly black hair. C. J. knew she was staring, but couldn't stop. It wasn't the woman's physical attractiveness that stunned her, although that in itself wasn't bad. It was her sheer presence. C. J. could almost touch the confidence that emanated from this woman. C. J. tried to recall what she had intended to say.

4

"Your name." The officer was waiting for her response. C. J. could only stare.

"Let me see your operator's license." She extended her hand. C. J. fought the urge to take hold of it. Somehow she managed to transfer the license to the officer. "C. J. Riley." The woman looked at her closely before asking, "What does the *C* stand for?" She tapped her pen against the citation pad.

The question brought C. J. back to earth. Few people outside her immediate family knew what her real name was, and absolutely no one used it. "C. J. will do. It was good enough for the state of Texas to use on my license, so I'm sure it'll serve your purpose." Having only her initials on her license had cost her two season tickets to the Dallas Cowboys, but it had been worth it.

The officer frowned. "I'm not concerned with the requirements for the state of Texas. I limit my concern to the city of San Antonio, and I'm required to fill in a name. So once more, Ms. Riley, what does the *C* stand for?"

Damn, C. J. thought, *I'll bet she sleeps with a rule book under her pillow.* C. J. instinctively changed tactics. The cop was a woman, and she hadn't met a woman yet, lesbian or not, who could resist her charms when she decided to turn them on. "It's just C. J.," she said with a warm smile. "Look, I may have been a little over the speed limit ..."

"Try eighty-five in a sixty-mile-per-hour zone."

"Okay." C. J. laughed and leaned against the Jag, striking her best pose. "You've got me, but I really can explain. I have a hot date tonight and she," C. J. paused to make sure the emphasis on *she* was processed. *Ah,* she smiled to herself, *the lady didn't blush or panic.* "Well, you know how upset the little woman can get when you're late. It wasn't really my fault. The board meeting with my father, Carlton Riley, ran late." *May as well let her know she's not dealing with just anyone here,* C. J. thought with smug satisfaction. Riley Produce was known throughout most of the United States. The use of Carlton Riley's name was guaranteed to smooth over any problem that she would encounter in Central or South Texas.

The officer's frown deepened as she shifted her weight to one leg. "Ms. Riley, I don't have the slightest interest in your love life or your father, but I'm sure the *little woman* and *Carlton Riley* would prefer you late rather than dead or seriously injured in an accident." She was taking information from C. J.'s license.

C. J. blinked in amazement as the cars continued to flash by them. This woman actually intended to give her a ticket. Maybe she was new to San Antonio and didn't know who Carlton Riley was, C. J. reasoned, pushing away from the car. There was a subtle shift in the officer's stance. C. J. sensed the woman's sense of alertness. In a dangerous situation, she wouldn't hesitate to react. C. J. found this alluring.

"You're not seriously considering giving me a ticket, are you? I mean, why bother? You do know who I am, don't you?"

The woman started to speak, but paused and gave C. J. a long look before replying. "You're just another traffic violation."

C. J. wondered briefly what the woman had started to say, but the scratching of her pen interrupted

C. J.'s musing. Exasperated, C. J. sighed and slapped the top of her car.

Her dad was going to be royally pissed if he found out about this ticket. He would start harping about *responsibility* again. He had nagged her for a week over that little dent she had put in the car at the mall last month. Hell, it wasn't her fault the guy had parked so screwy. How was she supposed to know his front end would be sticking out when she rounded the corner? Her own car had been in the shop for three days. She had been forced to stay home because she absolutely refused to drive the rental the insurance company offered. And she would be caught dead in her father's Civic. She made up her mind. He was not going to find out about this ticket.

"Look," she began, turning to face the officer. "I'm just going to take it to my father's lawyer and he'll do whatever needs to be done to get it fixed. So why waste our time and tax payer dollars?"

A deep frown creased the woman's forehead. Seeing this was the wrong tactic to take with her, C. J. quickly reined in her anger. "Come on." She lowered her voice and smiled. "Let's just forget this and let me take you somewhere nice for dinner."

The officer scribbled furiously, yanked the sheet away from the pad, and extended it to her.

This wasn't working. If the woman wanted to power trip, she'd let her. C. J. put on her best humble face. "Officer" — C. J. read the badge that was pinned above a very inviting and slightly heaving breast — "Franklin, you're absolutely right. I should be ashamed. I was acting like a spoiled brat." She smiled that perfect smile that was meant to melt stone. "Please. Let me make it up to you with dinner. I'll take the ticket." She took the ticket and slipped it into her pant's pocket, having no intention of paying it.

"What about the *little woman* at home?" Franklin asked as she slid the citation book into her hip pocket and clipped the pen to her shirt. "I thought she got angry if you were late."

Confident that she had found the right angle to handle her, C. J. stepped closer. "I'll just call and tell her I've managed to get myself arrested by the most gorgeous woman in Texas." She winked. "Maybe later you and I can find a use for those cute little handcuffs you're wearing." C. J. moved in still closer.

Franklin stepped in quickly to meet her. She was at least five-nine, a good two inches taller than C. J., but her scowl made it seem like a foot. Her voice was deep with anger when she replied. "Ms. Riley, the only reason these *cute* little handcuffs will ever get near you will be to haul your arrogant . . . self downtown. Before we reach that point, let me suggest that you crawl back into your car and go home. Because quite frankly it would give me a great deal of pleasure to know that you were spending a few hours in a holding cell cooling your rich little heels!"

Surprised, C. J. stepped back and blinked. No one ever talked to her like that. She quickly hid behind the shield she had built so carefully. "Ah," she cooed, "you really do love me." With exaggerated ease she slid behind the wheel and closed the door. The tinted window slid down quietly. "Until we meet again." She winked and blew Franklin a kiss.

Without warning she gunned the engine and left in a rush of squealing tires and burning rubber. She

8

watched in her rearview mirror as Franklin jumped into her car and tore out after her.

C. J. signaled and merged calmly into traffic and was careful to keep the Jag's speedometer at a sedate and legal sixty. Franklin trailed her until C. J. exited the freeway. C. J. watched as the patrol car disappeared down the road. "What a woman," she murmured. "I'll bet she's a hellcat in bed."

She chuckled as she turned the car around and headed toward home. She would call Anne tomorrow and make some kind of excuse. Right now she wanted to be alone to think about how she was going to capture the heart of Officer Franklin. The combination of her charm with the wealth and influence of Carlton Riley would make it a simple matter. *Hey, wasn't it always?*

She roared back onto the freeway, daydreaming of Officer Franklin lying in wait for her.

C. J. awoke the next morning tired and irritable. An elusive dark-haired beauty had invaded her sleep. In her dream C. J. would reach for and almost touch Officer Franklin before she inched farther away. Disgusted, she threw back the bedcovers and padded naked to the bathroom to start the shower. The mirror revealed dark circles under her eyes.

"What you need is a day in the sun," she mumbled, reaching for the phone. When the sleepy voice answered, she said, "Ron, C. J. How about a few games of tennis?" She knew she could count on Ron being ready to play. His lover, James, was a high-level executive for Taos Oil and Gas, and Ron's sole purpose in life was to stay home and look gorgeous for him.

He yawned loudly. "Sounds great, but couldn't you have waited until a decent hour? What time is it anyway?"

C. J. glanced at the clock. "It's a little after ten."

"God," he groaned. "Give me a couple of hours," C. J. knew he had been sleeping. "Let's go over to the new courts on Jasper. There's this absolutely scrumptious pro over there. If I have to get up at this ungodly hour, I may as well find a way to distract myself."

"Wouldn't that bother James?" C. J. squeezed toothpaste onto the toothbrush.

"Why? I'll be here looking radiant and available when he gets home."

"Ron, you're disgusting," C. J. teased. "No messing around, though. I really want a couple of good games."

"Uh-oh. Are you feeling your age this morning? Did some young thing toss you aside last night?"

"Fuck you," she growled around the toothbrush and hung up the phone. Ron never let her forget that he was four years younger. There were times when C. J. wondered why she liked him. Maybe it was because they had similar backgrounds and were both totally without ambition.

After showering, C. J. dressed in shorts and a knit shirt. She ran downstairs for breakfast and was surprised to find her father sitting at the table drinking a cup of coffee. C. J. knew he would have eaten breakfast hours ago. And usually at this time of day he was either at his office or off on one of his buying trips.

10

At fifty-nine Carlton Riley was still a handsome man. A healthy thatch of brown hair held thick streaks of gray at the temples. His strong face was tanned from endless hours in the sun. He loved visiting the growers and walking over the fields of produce, and he still did a lot of the buying for the company. Tiny squint lines were etched permanently at the edges of his eyes. Strong white teeth were displayed on those rare occasions when he would laugh. C. J. remembered him laughing a lot before her mother died.

People were always telling her how much she looked like her father. It was a fact she was proud of. There were times when she wished she could be more like him in other ways. He loved his work with a fire and passion that she had never been able to feel for anything. He had built Riley Produce from a small home-delivery business to a multimillion-dollar company.

At twenty-eight, C. J. still resided with him in her childhood home. She had never had to work, even though she currently held a token position as vice president, customer relations, of Riley Produce. The job required her to attend the Tuesday and Thursday board meetings, to listen to her father and four other board members discuss issues that didn't interest her in the slightest, and to sign a stack of letters that Janice, her father's secretary, wrote to customers who had written the company.

Other than Tuesdays and Thursdays, she was rarely in the office. She had worked out a system years ago with her father's secretary. Janice would slip her a piece of paper explaining in very brief detail what issues were going to be discussed at each meeting. And if seriously pushed, C. J. could babble something semi-intelligent. At the monthly wrap-up meeting she would quickly scan a report, prepared by Janice, that gave a statistical breakdown of customer concerns during the preceding month, and she would make a brief presentation from that information.

C. J. was sure the other company officers resented her, but she could care less. They were just jealous because she had a life and they were stuck in a stuffy office.

Life had always been the same for C. J. If she saw something she wanted, she used one of the credit cards her father gave her and someone paid the bills. Work was a concept that had no true meaning for her. There had been a time when her father tried to draw her into the business, but after years with no interest shown on her part, he had finally given up. He insisted she hold this position to ensure, as he liked to joke, that she would at least know where his office was.

The only other thing he had ever required her to do was finish college so she would have the skills necessary should she ever change her mind. C. J. had long been aware that she was a major disappointment to her father, and she often felt that her personality was flawed and that she lacked the essential element for success. She pushed the uncomfortable thoughts away.

"Why are you still home?" she asked, kissing him on the cheek before sitting down. The housekeeper appeared with coffee and toast, C. J.'s usual breakfast.

"I have to fly to Dallas later for a meeting, but a shipment of rose bushes came in and I want to get them planted before I leave." He placed a large hand around his coffee cup.

C. J. shook her head fondly. "Dad, you have a full-time gardener. Why don't you let him take care of the roses?"

"Because I enjoy working with the plants." He looked at her and offered a small smile. "Sometimes I think if I could do it all over I'd have become a gardener."

C. J. looked at him in mock horror. "I'd be driving a truck instead of my Jag?" She saw the worried frown slide over his face and was instantly sorry for her levity. She knew he felt responsible for her lack of ambition. "I was just joking, Dad."

"I know." He sighed. "You never take anything seriously, C. J."

"Let's not start this again, okay?" she sighed and searched for a safer subject. "I'm going to meet Ron for tennis later." Tennis was the one thing she felt good at.

"How is Ron?"

"Fine, still complaining that James is working too hard, but that's nothing new." C. J. had announced her lesbianism to her father when she was seventeen. He had been concerned at first and tried to get her to go to counseling, but she had stubbornly refused. Over the years he seemed to adjust and had silently watched her move from woman to woman, with nothing more than an occasional frown and one short lecture on the feelings of others. This occurred after the household had been disrupted for a month by one of C. J.'s jilted lovers, who believed C. J.'s interest would return if she called or dropped by enough.

"So what's new in your life?" he asked, sipping his coffee.

"Nothing really."

"I never see you. Our paths don't seem to cross very often."

"That's because you work too hard," C. J. scolded as she finished off her toast. She suddenly thought of Officer Franklin.

"Dad." She played with the crumbs on the plate, pushing them into a tiny pile in the center with her finger. "How did you know you loved Mom?" Seeing his surprised look she continued quickly. "What I mean is, why her rather than someone else?" C. J. wondered if she was capable of falling in love. She had dated and slept with more women than she wanted to remember, and although she had cared for them at the time, she couldn't honestly say she had loved any of them.

C. J. smiled, and his eyes softened as memories slipped back through time. "I knew the minute I saw her that she was the woman for me. Unfortunately, she didn't."

C. J.'s attention perked. "She wasn't interested in you?" She couldn't fathom a heterosexual woman who wasn't interested in him. There had certainly been plenty trying to catch his attention since her mother's death, but her father had always seemed oblivious to them.

He laughed at her surprise. "You never knew your grandparents. They died when you were just a baby. My father was very strict. He believed in the man being the head of the household and ruling with an iron hand." He stopped and glanced at her. "Maybe that's why I was so lax with you."

He shook his head and picked up his story. "I was being groomed to step into the banking business with my father. The only problem was, I enjoyed digging in the dirt of a garden more than the dirt of Wall Street and banking. My father wanted to stick me behind a desk with ledgers and balance sheets, but I refused. After I graduated from college, I rebelled and went to work as a sales manager for Stapleton's Produce."

He chuckled and shook his head. "Your mother worked in the billing office. I kept asking her out, and she kept refusing. He shrugged as if embarrassed. "I guess I was used to getting my own way, and for the life of me I couldn't figure out what there was about me your mother wouldn't like. After several futile attempts in asking her out, it finally dawned in my thick head to ask her why." He sipped his coffee before continuing. "She very politely informed me that I was a self-centered pompous ass."

"I can't imagine." C. J. shook her head. "You two always got along so well."

He rubbed his hand across his cheek. "Your mother was very good at reminding me that my father might be one of the most prominent bankers in Texas, but I still had plenty of human faults." Glancing at his watch he pushed his cup away. "I have to get started if I'm going to get those roses planted." He stood and kissed the top of her head. His hand rested on her shoulder. "Was there a reason for that question? Someone special maybe?"

C. J.'s mind filled with a vision of Officer Franklin, and a strange feeling accompanied that vision. She shrugged it off and admonished herself. "Hey," she boasted, "you know me better than that. I'm not the marrying kind."

She stared at the table, knowing that if she looked up his eyes would be filled with concern, wondering where he had gone wrong. He patted her shoulder. "I'll see you when I get back from Dallas, or at Tuesday's meeting for sure."

C. J. sat staring into her now cold coffee thinking about Officer Franklin.

Ron was already on the court warming up with some man when she arrived. She stood watching them. Ron was short, with a baby face that would forever conceal his real age. The sun glinted off his blond, precisely trimmed hair. He saw her as he lunged for a burning drive.

"You're late." He shook a finger at C. J. before throwing an exaggerated kiss to the man who coyly caught it and hurried away. "Isn't he absolutely adorable?" Ron sighed and joined her as they watched the retreating figure.

"Not as cute as James."

"Don't be catty. Besides, when did you become the keeper of the morality key?" He patted his face with a towel.

She shrugged. "I don't have serious relationships. You know I make that clear at the very beginning."

"Sure, like those dear hearts actually listen to you. Every one of them believes she's going to be the one who tames the great C. J. Riley."

"I'm not responsible for what other people think," she snapped. She squinted into the sun. "Are we going to play tennis, or are you going to talk me to death?"

Ron tossed the towel onto a bench and returned to his side of the net. "Oh my, we are grumpy today, aren't we? What's the story behind those Gucci bags under your eyes?"

"Rough night." She absently bounced a tennis ball.

"Ooh, Ms. Anne keep you up all night, did she?"

"I didn't make it over there." C. J. remembered she still hadn't called Anne. "I got a speeding ticket on the way to her place. By then I was so late I decided to go back home." The ball made hollow thuds against the court.

"A ticket!" he squealed. "That's new. What happened? Normally you pull that Carlton-Riley's-my-daddy routine and they end up apologizing for being an inconvenience to you." Suspicion filled his curious eyes. "What's the real story?"

She looked at him and started grinning. "The traffic cop was this great-looking woman."

Ron shrieked. "Whew. You go, girl. Slumming with a city servant! Those working stiffs do have a certain appeal."

She snatched the ball out of the air, his attitude suddenly grating on her. It was nothing new for them to make fun of the working stiffs, as they referred to anyone who pulled the nine-to-five routine, the only exceptions being her father and James. "Shut up," she growled as she knelt to re-tie her shoes. "She was just doing her job."

He ran up to the net. "Whoa, do I detect a note of caring here? Let me call a doctor. If C. J. Riley is having an attack of feelings, there must be something seriously wrong."

"Cut it out. I was just yanking your chain." She

17

stood and pulled her racket from the case and tossed the case onto a bench. "Are we going to play or bullshit all day?" She threw the ball at him. "You serve."

They played two sets. She took both six-love.

She showered and changed into clothes she had brought along. Ron rushed off to another appointment. She wondered briefly if he was meeting the pro somewhere. She had never thought about Ron cheating on James. They had never discussed it. She tried to remember how long he and James had been together — five or six years.

She and Ron had met in college at Trinity University. She had been a senior, he a freshman. They had hit if off immediately. Neither ever intended to work and, thanks to their families' money, neither ever expected to have to.

During Ron's sophomore year he had been caught in a rather compromising position with another male student. Ron's father disowned him, leaving him to fend for himself. A few months later Ron moved in with James, who was ten years older and made plenty of money to provide for Ron's expensive tastes.

C. J. climbed into the Jag and roared from the parking lot. She had to do something about Anne. *Maybe it's time to move on*, she thought. The only reason she had put up with Anne's bullshit this long was because she was so good in bed and had never nagged C. J. about a *forever relationship*. Again she thought of Officer Franklin. She had to find a way to see her again.

C. J. was almost home before the idea hit her. Grabbing the phone she called a woman she once dated. The woman now worked as a dispatcher for the

City of San Antonio Police Department. A few weeks earlier, the city had launched a massive campaign against speeding. The police department had been warning drivers that additional patrol cars would be posted around the city. Franklin was sure to be patrolling somewhere.

It cost her fifty bucks, but within minutes she knew the exact location and time that Officer Lois Franklin would be waiting for unsuspecting speeders. Looking at her watch, she saw she still had a couple of hours to kill. She drove to Rosenbloom's Jewelry where Anne had seen the earrings she wanted. Anne was a struggling artist, but with her trust fund she would never be required to struggle too much.

At the jewelry store, a short brunette with steel gray eyes met C. J. at the counter. "May I help you?" Her gaze traveled slowly down C. J.'s body.

C. J. flashed her an automatic I'll-take-anything-you're-offering smile. "I'm interested in a pair of earrings I saw here a few weeks ago."

"The small jade drops?"

C. J. blinked in surprised. "Yeah. How did you remember?"

"I'd never forget you." She ran her hand down C. J.'s arm as she lowered her lashes. "Follow me."

C. J. felt the heat between her legs grow as she watched the seductive sway of the woman's hips. By the time they had reached the display where the earrings were, C. J. had almost forgotten why she had come in.

The woman unlocked the case and held one of the earrings up. C. J. enclosed the woman's hand with both of hers.

"Wouldn't want to drop it," she said, staring into the woman's eyes.

As she pretended to examine the earring, C. J. took the opportunity to see who else was in the store. There was only one other clerk, and he was busy arranging a window display.

The woman's hand rested on her arm. "Someone's a very lucky woman," she pouted. C. J. had to resist jumping over the counter.

"I'll take these. Can you have them delivered?" She gave her Anne's studio address and a credit card. As the woman prepared the earrings, C. J. wrote and enclosed a card. She apologized for missing their date and promised to make it up to her many times over. As C. J. signed the credit card receipt, the woman leaned toward her.

"I have an item in the back that might interest you."

C. J. could feel the woman's breath on her cheek and could smell her seductive perfume. "I want to see everything you have to offer," C. J. murmured and let her lips brush across the woman's cheek.

"I'll be right back," the woman called to the man at the window. He looked over his shoulder at C. J. and gave a slight smile.

C. J. followed her into a small office and closed the door. She pulled the woman to her and leaned against the door as she greedily kissed her way down the woman's throat. The woman moaned as C. J. unbuttoned the woman's blouse and pushed it away. She let her tongue trace the edges around the thin lace bra. She slipped the woman's skirt off and trailed her hands up the back of her legs. The woman tugged C. J.'s shirt from her shorts. C. J. caught the woman's hands and pulled them gently behind the woman as she kissed her. As the tongues entwined, C. J. could feel the woman's desire grow. With a sense of urgency they undressed.

C. J.'s lips encircled a hardened nipple and sucked greedily.

"Now," the woman moaned. C. J. moved to her lips and kissed her deeply. Her pulse raced. This was the only time she ever felt needed. She lived for these moments when she could drive some woman to the point of no return. To the point to where for a few precious moments, some woman needed her more than anything else did on earth.

Her mouth reclaimed a breast as her hand slid between the woman's thighs. Slowly C. J. moved her toward a littered desk a few feet away. Once there, C. J. picked the woman up and laid her across it. She spread the woman's legs and stood between them, leaning over and kissing her deeply before working her way down her stomach. The woman's hands were on her head urging her down. The woman arched against her as C. J. slipped a finger deep inside. C. J.'s heart soared as the woman came with a series of loud groans that C. J. was certain anyone in the store would be able to hear.

C. J. again leaned over her and let her hand continue to tease her wetness. "You're right," she breathed as she nuzzled her neck. "I do like the items back here much better." When C. J. pulled her lips away to capture a tempting nipple, the woman sighed. "I only have a few minutes. Let me taste you." She started to sit up, but C. J. placed her hands on the woman's shoulders and pressed her back down. "Didn't your boss ever tell you you're supposed to keep the customer happy?" C. J. teased.

"That's exactly what I'm trying to do," the woman cooed.

"Then lie back," C. J. murmured. C. J.'s hand slid between the woman's legs and began a steady stroking. The woman's hands tightened around C. J.'s back, and the warm feeling began to envelop C. J. until she felt she would implode from it. When the woman came in a burst of loud exclamations, C. J. felt her own body explode with the pleasure of being wanted.

With a smile and wink the woman quickly dressed. She pointed out the restroom to C. J. before going back to the showroom. C. J. took her time in the restroom before following her. As C. J. walked through the showroom, the woman was with another customer. "I hope you enjoyed your visit," she said, tossing her a coy smile.

C. J. licked her lips. "Yes. Everything was very tasteful. Thanks for showing me your special merchandise."

"I hope you'll come again," the woman said, arching her eyebrows.

Driving away from the jewelry store, C. J. called a floral shop and had a large bouquet of roses sent to Anne's studio and another one to Anne's apartment. With her conscience soothed, she turned up the volume on her CD player and headed in search of Officer Franklin.

The police car was parked at the end of a curve. C. J. saw it in plenty of time to increase her speed enough to catch Franklin's attention. The speedometer was registering an even eighty as she flew by, and, as she had hoped, the reaction was immediate. The car pulled out behind her, lights flashing. C. J. slowed to make sure Franklin would be able to catch up, and, after a few seconds, she pulled to the shoulder.

She retrieved her driver's license from the visor and opened the car door. In slow, exaggerated moves she got out. Officer Franklin was already beside her.

"Operator's license please," she stated bluntly. She took the license and began filling out the citation.

"No, hello C. J., nice to see you again? Why, Officer Franklin, you disappoint me. I thought you'd be glad to see me." C. J. pulled off her sunglasses and caught the musky scent of the woman from the jewelry store on her hand. For a moment she felt a strange sense of guilt, but brushed it away. She wasn't committed to anyone.

"You were driving eighty in a sixty-mile-per-hour zone. Please sign here." She extended the citation pad and pen.

C. J. reached for them, taking both of Franklin's hands into hers. Franklin jerked away. "I don't bite . . . hard," C. J. said with a suggestive wink before signing the citation and handing it and the pen back. "Have dinner with me, please."

"I have a job to do. Which is something you wouldn't understand."

The jab hurt more than it should have, so C. J.

pushed it away. Why should she care what this woman thought about her? She was just jealous like everyone else. C. J. had discovered many years before how to hide pain. When you grew up never fitting in, you learned to adjust.

"You are interested in me. You went to the trouble to find out something about me," C. J. teased. She smiled her best smile. "I could tell you much more over dinner."

Franklin shook her head and hooked her thumbs in her pistol belt. "I already know more than I want to about you. Your speeding prowess seems to be well known throughout most precincts in town. It's amazing you're still allowed to drive."

"Not everyone is as conscientious as you are, Officer Franklin. But under your tutelage I'm sure I can learn to change my bad habits. Why don't we discuss it further over dinner?"

"Good day, Ms. Riley." Franklin turned and walked to her patrol car.

"Nice to see you again." C. J. waved as the patrol car pulled back onto the road. She stood for several seconds staring at the disappearing car. Officer Franklin was going to be a challenge, and it had been a long time since C. J. had had a good challenge.

CHAPTER TWO

C. J. dropped the wet towel to the floor and strolled naked into her bedroom. She placed another call to her friend at the police department. For the price of two front-row tickets to an upcoming concert, she had Officer Lois Franklin's full name, home address, phone number, and the time she would be coming off duty today.

C. J. had briefly pondered why she was trying so hard with this woman. It wasn't normal for her. Women chased her. She didn't have to bother. That must be it, she reasoned as she pulled clothes from her closet. The excitement of the chase was in her blood.

She tugged the legs of her black Levi's down over the silver-tipped western boots. With an economy of movement she tucked the tail of the white cotton shirt into her jeans and added a black leather vest. A few swipes of a comb though her short brown hair and she was on her way out.

The police substation where Lois Franklin worked was south of downtown. C. J. refused to let the Friday evening traffic dampen her spirit. Tonight was the night. She could feel it. Lois Franklin wouldn't resist her if she were off duty. She had probably been ignoring her because of her corny sense of responsibility while in uniform. C. J. whistled a happy tune. Twenty minutes later, she was leaning against the Jag as a group of loud voices emerged from the police station. Several men and a couple of women tried to catch her attention, but C. J. ignored them. There was only one person who held any interest for her right now.

Lois Franklin didn't exit the building until twenty-seven minutes later. C. J. knew exactly how late she was because she had watched each minute slip by with anxious anticipation.

When Franklin appeared she was wearing faded denim jeans with a red cotton button-down shirt. A light denim jacket was flung over her shoulder. A slight smile was playing across her face, and C. J. felt something inside her twist sharply. She had difficulty breathing as she watched the muscles in Lois Franklin's thighs move beneath the tight denim.

Franklin was less than ten feet away before she noticed C. J. The look of surprise was followed swiftly by the ever-present frown.

"Good evening, Officer Franklin." C. J. felt sure the entire substation could hear her heart pounding. Why was this woman having such an effect on her?

"Ms. Riley. You should mail your speeding violation charges to the address on the citation," she said in a tight voice.

"And miss spending time with you? Never."

Franklin turned away. "Good evening, Ms. Riley."

C. J. ran to her side. "Lois wait. That's no —"

Franklin whirled around. "How do you know my name?"

C. J. stuttered, realizing she had made a mistake. This wasn't a woman to push. "You signed the ticket," she tried lamely.

"I only use my first initial, and how did you know where to find me tonight?" Franklin was in C. J.'s face. "Do you know stalking is a crime?"

"Stalking!" C. J. sputtered. This woman thought that she, C. J. Riley, would have to stalk a woman to get her attention. She felt her anger building. "I found you attractive, Officer Franklin. Rather than stalking you, I simply took the time and effort to find you while you were off duty to let you know I'm interested in you."

"Is this where I'm supposed to drop to my knees and thank you for bestowing such wonders upon me?" Franklin snapped as she jabbed C. J.'s shoulder with her finger.

"There are hundreds of women who would definitely consider that an honor," C. J. blazed back, leaning closer to her.

"Well, do me and those hundred other women a favor and turn your attention to them." Franklin was so close C. J. could see the tiny, dark flecks in her light blue eyes. They were the color of blue that appears at the hottest part of a flame or, as they now looked, the deepest cold of ice.

Without knowing how it really happened, C. J. found her lips pressed against Franklin's. For the barest moment she felt a response before Franklin yanked away. The flurry of sensation ripping through C. J. was dashed by a resounding slap. C. J. staggered in surprise and felt her boot heel catch on a broken spot in the pavement. As she fell backward she saw a kaleidoscope of emotions wash across Lois Franklin's face — anger, shock, and fear as she grabbed for C. J.'s falling body and missed. C. J.'s head struck the Jag's fender, and a multitude of stars exploded.

C. J. opened her eyes to the face of a strange man.

"Welcome back, Ms. Riley," he said with a smile. "I'm Dr. Morgan. You're at the Southeast Baptist emergency room. Now let's just take a look." He pulled C. J.'s eyelid up and flashed a light into her eyes. After repeating the movement with her other eye, he moved back to the first one. Annoyed and embarrassed at her clumsiness, C. J. pushed him away.

"I'm fine, just a slight headache." She turned her head and instantly regretted the movement. As the pain cleared she saw Lois Franklin standing beside her. Franklin appeared to be engrossed in studying the floor.

This is bullshit, C. J. thought, her head pounding in pain. She had never chased a woman, and she could damn well do without Lois Franklin. No one was worth this much trouble. But there was still a part of her that screamed that Lois Franklin was definitely worth the trouble. Irritated, she lashed out with the sarcasm that had always been her main protection against things that hurt her.

"Officer Franklin, do you always settle your differences with such violence?" C. J. asked, rubbing her head.

Franklin blushed crimson as she looked into C. J.'s eyes. C. J. couldn't help but notice how beautiful she was.

"I'm sorry you fell. I tried to catch you." Franklin looked nervously at the doctor.

"I believe the term for what we shared was police brutality," C. J. insisted, not willing to forgive the humiliation Lois was causing her.

"Police brutality! Damn your arrogant hide. If you hadn't . . ." Franklin stopped, took a deep breath, and slowly exhaled before turning to the doctor. "Will you be keeping her overnight?"

"No, I'm not staying overnight," C. J. insisted. She had to force herself not to grab her aching head as she sat up.

The doctor stared at C. J. "Well, as long as there's someone to watch her, and if she agrees to check in tomorrow with her own physician, it shouldn't be necessary for her to stay. It's just a nasty bump." He turned to C. J. "You'll have a headache for a couple of days."

"I'm fine," C. J. insisted.

"Then tell me who to call to drive you home," Lois said.

"I'll drive myself."

"No," the doctor and Lois answered in unison.

The doctor shook his head. "Under no circumstance can I release you if you're going to be driving."

C. J. ran through her list of possibilities. Her father was out of town. Ron would be with James and would piss and moan for days if she bothered him. Anne probably wasn't speaking to her yet. She could call Alice, the housekeeper, but she was still in a huff over their spat about the dry cleaning.

"I'll drive you home," Lois said, interrupting C. J.'s thoughts.

"I'll walk. Or better yet, I'll call a cab."

"Absolutely not, Ms. Riley." the doctor said. "The hospital could not take that responsibility. I'll only release you if I know there's someone willing to be responsible for you. Even if there's no concussion, head injuries are nothing to take lightly. You should be watched very closely for the next twenty-four hours."

If my father wasn't Carlton Riley, I'll bet you'd have no problem with that responsibility, C. J. thought with bitterness.

"Look." Lois slapped her hands against her thighs. "For all I care you can spend the night here. It seems pretty obvious that there's no one else to pick you up. Since I do feel somewhat responsible, I'll drive you home."

"Somewhat responsible. If you hadn't hit me . . ."

The doctor shuffled uncomfortably.

"Fine. Stay." Lois turned to leave the room.

"Wait." C. J. knew she'd rather beg Lois for a ride than spend a night in a hospital. Her mother had gone to the hospital when C. J. was twelve and had never returned home. "You can drive me home. The housekeeper will be there." *I could learn to hate this woman*, C. J. growled to herself.

Twenty minutes later, a nurse wheeled a still grumbling C. J. down the hall. Through the large double doors, C. J. could see Lois leaning against a huge monster of a truck. Its oversize tires raised it high above the ground.

The March night air must have turned cool, because Lois was now wearing the denim jacket she had been carrying earlier. The wind was blowing her hair across her face. She kept tossing her head irritably to keep it out of her eyes.

C. J. watched her and suddenly felt like a gallon of warm molasses was running through her veins. What was it about this woman? C. J.'s breath was coming in short gasps, and a fine sweat broke out over her body.

"Are you all right?" the nurse asked. She took C. J.'s wrist to check her pulse, but C. J. pulled away. If the nurse checked her vital signs now, they would surely keep her at the hospital.

C. J. looked back out at Lois and was struck by a moment of insight. She couldn't honestly say she had ever loved anyone other than her parents, but for a short terrifying moment she acknowledged she might be falling in love with Lois Franklin. She allowed herself to relive the short kiss, then touched the knot on the back of her head and winced. It was almost worth it.

Watching Lois standing there so self-assured, C. J. was struck by the harsh fact that maybe there were some things that even Carlton Riley's money couldn't buy. She wondered how people without the benefits of power and money survived. If these attributes didn't have an effect on Lois, then how would she ever convince her that she was falling in love with her?

The hospital doors slid open, and the nurse wheeled C. J. out. Lois pushed away from the truck and opened the passenger door. C. J. sat in the wheelchair and stared at the truck. Its enormous tires made for a three-foot step up.

"I guess it's rather high," Lois said, pushing her hands down into her pockets. "If you like I could give you a boost in."

"I can make it fine," C. J. insisted. She stood and made a rather ungraceful climb up into the big, black monster. Lois closed the door before going around to the other side and hopping in behind the wheel in one fluid motion.

"Where's my car?" C. J. asked, trying to place the pleasant but elusive smell that filled the cab of the truck.

"Still at the station. You can have it picked up tomorrow."

C. J.'s reflection stared back at her from the tinted window. She couldn't resist nettling Lois. "Tell me, Officer Franklin, does this machine represent your darker, violent side?"

Lois exhaled a long sigh. "I'm sorry I hit you. I don't know where that came from. I swear it's not something I've ever done before."

C. J. turned toward her. "I guess I should be grateful you weren't still on duty. You would've probably shot me."

"Damn you!" Lois leaned into the steering wheel and glared at her. "Don't you understand anything? It's that juvenile attitude of yours that pisses me off. Yes, I work for a living. I'm not a rich little brat like you who sees everything as a big joke or a personal toy you can play with until you grow bored and decide to dump it."

"You're very beautiful when you're angry."

Lois shook her head. "You are beyond hope. What's your address? The sooner I get you home the better." She turned the key, and the powerful engine sprang to life.

C. J. wasn't ready to let Lois get away. "What about dinner? I'm starving."

"Your housekeeper will be glad to feed you."

"I lied. It's her night off." C. J. flashed her a wicked smile.

Lois frowned. "Will someone be at the house with you tonight?"

"If I say no, can I convince you to stay and keep me warm?"

"You say no, and I'll haul your butt back inside," she said, nodding toward the hospital entrance.

"Okay, you win. Drag me back home. Condemn me to a cold, lonely bed."

"I seriously doubt your bed is ever cold."

"Oh, was that curiosity or mere speculation?" C. J. teased.

"Neither. Where to?"

C. J. was hit by a wave of loneliness. She didn't want to go home. She gave her Anne's address. Maybe the earrings and flowers had softened her anger.

Lois frowned as she shifted the truck into gear. "That's not the address on your license."

"You memorized my address?" C. J. felt her heart miss a beat. "Then there's hope for us."

"You are unbelievable." Lois sighed again and pulled into traffic. "Is this a valid address? I'm really beat and honestly don't feel like driving you all over the city."

C. J. studied Lois's face in the pale light from the panel. She did look tired. "It's a valid address." She felt a need to do something for this woman. But somehow the usual flowers and gifts seemed wrong. What would Lois Franklin want? "Being a cop is hard work, huh?" she asked.

Lois shrugged in the semidarkness of the truck. "Some days are worse than others."

"Why did you become a cop?" C. J. wanted to learn everything there was to know about her.

"I wasn't born rich, and I had to work."

C. J. flinched and turned back to stare out the window. The comment had hurt. "Why does everyone think it's so damn great to be born rich?" They were driving through the edge of downtown, and C. J.'s eyes rested for a brief moment on a homeless man standing in a darkened doorway.

"Maybe you'd rather change places with that guy," Lois said, nodding to the homeless man.

C. J. was ashamed of her whining. She should be grateful for what she had, but there were times when she wished her father was just a regular guy who worked at a mill or something. Someone who had come home at five every afternoon. She kept her face turned away.

"I'm sorry," Lois said. "It's just that I never know if you're serious or about to bombard me again with your witless humor."

"Forget it." C. J.'s head was throbbing, and Lois's words had cut deep. Why was she making such a fool of herself over this woman?

"C. J., I'm really sorry." Lois laid her hand on C. J.'s arm.

C. J. stared at the hand. She was making a fool of herself over this woman. She didn't need Lois Franklin or anyone else. She took Lois's hand into her own and began to caress it. Lois tried to pull away, but C. J. held firm. She wanted to hurt Lois, the way her remark had hurt. "Do you think playing hard to get will make me want you more?" C. J. could hear the cruelty in her voice but couldn't stop it. "A one-night stand was all I was looking for, *Officer* Franklin," she sneered.

Lois jerked her hand away, causing the truck to swerve. A horn blasted angrily beside her. "You . . ." Lois's voice shook with anger. "Do us both a favor and shut your mouth."

C. J. leaned back onto the seat and fell asleep.

C. J. woke up to Anne calling her name and shaking her. "Come on, baby. Wake up."

"What?" C. J.'s head was pounding. She tried to slip back into the comforting slumber.

"You're home." Lois Franklin's voice brought her eyes open.

"C. J., come on," Anne persisted. "I'll help you out." Anne's slight five-foot-two frame looked as though it would barely support itself. Both women towered over her.

"Let me help," Lois suggested.

C. J. bristled. She didn't need anything from anybody, and certainly not Lois Franklin. "Get back. I can do it myself. Don't they train you people in anything now?" C. J. growled at Lois.

"Now what?" Lois asked, placing her hands on her hips.

"I have a head injury," C. J. replied sarcastically. "Everyone knows you shouldn't have let me fall asleep."

Lois snorted and shot back. "You do what you please. Why should I waste my breath?"

Anne's snicker enraged C. J. further. She shrugged off Anne's hand. Anne stepped back, but Lois stepped forward and took a firm grip on C. J.'s arm as C. J. slid from the truck. The impact brought a fresh wave of pain to her head.

C. J.'s knees nearly buckled. "I can take care of myself," C. J. said and tried to pull away from Lois.

"Sure you can," Franklin quipped.

Angry beyond reason, C. J. reached into her pocket and removed a ten-dollar bill. "For your trouble, Officer Franklin. I know you poor city employees can barely make ends meet."

"C. J., stop it," Anne hissed.

C. J. felt Lois's body stiffen. "I can't accept that," Lois answered, pushing C. J.'s hand away.

"Sure you can. Consider it a tip for services rendered. The kiss alone was worth it."

Lois's face blazed scarlet.

Anne took C. J.'s arm. "That's enough," she snapped. "You're making a complete fool of yourself. Get inside and let me help you into bed."

C. J.'s head hurt, and Lois Franklin had rejected her. Anne was treating her like a child, and, like a spoiled child, she let her anger replace reason. "Now see Franklin, here is a woman with real class. My crawling into her bed can cost me a couple of thousand a week, but hell she's worth..."

C. J.'s statement was cut short when for the second time in one night she was soundly slapped. C. J. saw the pain and tears spring to Anne's eyes, and remorse raced through her. Anne hadn't deserved that cheap shot. Anne was already inside behind a closed door before either Lois or C. J. could react. C. J. thought of knocking on her door and apologizing, but knew she'd just look like a bigger fool.

"Looks like it's just you and me, baby," C. J. said and climbed back into the truck feeling like a complete ass.

"What do you think you're doing?" Lois demanded. "Get out of my truck." Her voice shook with anger.

"I can't stay here. You'll have to drive me home. It's your civic duty, Officer Franklin." C. J. tried not to notice how beautiful Lois looked standing there with her hands planted firmly on her hips, her face glowing with anger. The woman reeked of barely restrained passion.

Lois rubbed her forehead, her ever-present frown deepening. "No," she said, running to the door where Anne had disappeared. She rang the doorbell and knocked for several minutes, but Anne failed to reappear.

Lois finally gave up and stormed back. "Where to?"

she demanded as she clambered back into the truck and slammed the door with such a vengeance that the vehicle rocked.

C. J. had to sit on her hands to keep from grabbing her head as pain shot through it. "You should know the address by heart," she offered. "You've written it enough recently."

"Cut the bullshit. I know it's in Alamo Heights, but that's not exactly my beat."

"Of course not. You would never dirty your shoe soles on such rich soil, would you?"

"Just give me the damn address, unless you want to go back to the hospital," Lois said and started the engine.

Exhausted, C. J. leaned back into the seat and gave her the address. She kept her eyes closed and pretended to sleep. She felt like shit, and it had nothing to do with her head. She had needlessly hurt Anne and had made a fool of herself in the process.

Eventually the truck slowed. The slight gasp from Franklin told C. J. she was home.

C. J. had been five when her parents bought this house. Her father had put a small fortune into renovating it. He and her mother had spent hours with contractors and blueprints. C. J. took the three-story house on a hill surrounded by five wooded acres for granted. It rarely, if ever, occurred to her that its fifteen rooms and large ballroom were merely a dream to most people. Knowing that Lois Franklin was impressed, she smiled with a warm glow of pride.

The truck came to a stop and the engine died. C. J. sat up.

"No need to trouble yourself with coming in,

Officer Franklin. I can make it from here." She opened the door and hopped to the ground. Once again, the impact caused a blinding pain to shoot through her head.

A warm hand took her arm. "I can see you're fine, Ms. Riley; however, I did give the doctor my word that I'd ensure you were watched during the night. If it's all the same to you, I'll just make sure before I leave."

"I'll bet you're real big on keeping promises," C. J. said as she started toward the house.

"Well, you know what they say, a promise is a promise."

C. J. was too weary to fight. Her head felt like it was going to fall off. Plus, she enjoyed the feel of Lois's hand on her arm and didn't want to say anything that would make her move it.

Lois was ringing the doorbell.

"I have a key," C. J. said, digging into her pockets.

"Forget it. I'm not leaving until I talk to someone."

Carlton Riley opened the door. "Dad!" C. J. Exclaimed and grabbed her aching head. "I thought you were out of town."

"The meeting was canceled," he said, staring at Lois, who was still holding C. J.'s arm.

C. J. took her hand from her head and motioned toward Lois. "Dad, this is Officer Lois Franklin. Officer Franklin, Carlton Riley, my father."

Lois released C. J.'s arm and extended her hand. "Nice to meet you, sir."

He stared back and forth between the women. "Officer Franklin," he finally acknowledged. He shook her hand and looked in the direction of the truck over C. J.'s shoulder before he asked. "Is there something wrong?"

"No, sir. Your daughter had a slight accident. The doctor wanted to make sure someone was here to watch her tonight."

"Accident? Doctor? C. J., are you okay?"

C. J. could see the panic in his eyes and deeply regretted being the cause of it. "I'm fine, Dad. It's nothing serious."

"Was anyone else hurt?" he asked.

"No, she fell," Lois offered.

C. J. knew the questions were about to begin, and she quickly headed them off.

"Since you weren't supposed to be home, Officer Franklin volunteered to watch over me tonight," she said.

C. J. saw Lois's face grow red at the insinuation.

Her father cleared his throat. "Oh," he said, flustered. "I'll leave you two alone then." He stepped away from the door.

Lois turned to leave. "Aren't you staying?" C. J. called after her, trying not to laugh at Lois's discomfort since it caused her head to hurt worse. "I'm a big girl. Dad knows I sleep with women."

"Not with this one, you don't," Lois hurled over her shoulder.

C. J.'s laughter sent a new ripple of pain through her head.

"What happened to you?" her father asked as she closed the door. "Where's your car?"

"It was nothing. I tripped and hit my head. Lois

didn't think I should be driving, so I'll pick up the car tomorrow."

"Let me see." He examined the knot on the back of her head. "Did you see a doctor?"

"Yeah." They walked toward his study. This was C. J.'s favorite room in the house. It was a small, comfortable room that was simply furnished. A dark blue sofa was against one wall with a large oak desk across from it. Bookshelves lined most of the remaining wall space. An overstuffed chair stood at an angle at the end of the sofa. A huge ottoman sat near it.

C. J. stretched out on the sofa. Her father sat in the chair.

"How did you fall?" he asked, propping his feet up on the ottoman.

"You don't want to know."

After a moment he sighed. "No. I suppose not."

She could feel him watching her. Uneasy with his scrutiny, she got up before he could ask more questions. "I'm going to bed."

She walked to the chair and kissed his cheek. The lamplight caught the gray in his hair. It occurred to her that he looked tired.

"Are you feeling all right?"

"Just tired," he assured her, squeezing her hand and picking up a stack of papers. C. J. realized he must have been working when she and Lois came in. She turned to leave.

"C. J., I'm sorry if she left because I was home."

"No, Dad, I was just razzing her. She's not the sleepover type."

The doorbell rang again. "Now what?" he asked, tossing his papers aside.

"I'll get it."

"No, go on up to bed." They crossed the foyer together. C. J. headed upstairs as her father opened the door.

She was halfway up when he called to her. "C. J., there's a package for you."

She started back down, frowning. "A package? It's after midnight. Who would send something this late?"

"I don't know. It came by special courier."

He was at the bottom of the stairs holding a small package. She opened it to find the jade earrings she had sent to Anne.

"Someone must be pretty serious to be sending you gifts like this," he said. He whistled as he picked one up.

"They're not for me," she confessed. "I gave them to someone. She's returning them." C. J. sat down heavily on the stairs. Anne wouldn't be forgiving her this time. She didn't love Anne, but they did have a lot in common. On their good days they had a lot of fun together. She would miss her.

An awkward silence fell between them. His hand squeezed her shoulder. "C. J., if your mother were here, she would know what to say." He paused. "Is there anything I can do? Maybe you should call this woman."

"No. I think this one is beyond repair. I'll see you tomorrow." She stood and started up the stairs.

He gave a loud sigh and headed back toward his study.

She crawled into bed feeling miserable. She had been cruel to Anne for no good reason, and Lois still wouldn't give her the time of day. But worst of all, she had disappointed her father again. She closed her eyes, exhausted. She promised herself that tomorrow she would call them both and apologize. But she doubted she'd ever be able to make her father proud of her.

CHAPTER THREE

Someone was pounding on the door. C. J. turned and pulled the pillow over her aching head.

"Miss Riley, get up." Alice, the housekeeper, had come in and was shaking her. "Get up."

"Leave me alone," she whined, pushing away the firm, slightly work-roughened hand.

"It's your father."

C. J. shot up and grabbed her aching head. "Dad. What's wrong?"

"He's sick and won't listen to me. You have to talk

some sense into him. Get up, please." C. J. could see the fear in the woman's eyes.

C. J. forgot the pain in her head as she grabbed her robe and raced downstairs behind Alice. They found Mr. Riley in the study sitting behind his desk. His face was a sickly gray, and his breath came in sharp gasps.

"Dad, what's wrong? Alice, call nine-one-one and get an ambulance here."

"No. I'm fine," he answered in a voice barely more than a whisper. Alice stopped, uncertain.

C. J. saw her hesitate. "Alice, move!" Alice left in a rush.

"C. J.," her father said, patting her hand. "Don't be so harsh on people. They do the best they can."

She took her father's hand between hers. It was clammy. Fear rose to a tight knot in her throat.

"I'm sorry, Dad. I'm worried about you." It seemed like she was always apologizing. Why couldn't she make him happy? Just once do something that would make him proud of her. Why hadn't she paid more attention to his exhaustion last night? *Because as usual I was too wrapped up in my own problems*, she chided herself.

It took the paramedics twelve long minutes to arrive. Alice met them and showed them to the study. C. J. watched in a daze as they hooked up a heart monitor and started an IV. C. J. felt the horror start deep in her gut. He was going to the hospital just as her mother had gone. She followed the stretcher out, but a paramedic stopped her at the ambulance door.

The young paramedic cleared his throat. "Sorry, ma'am. You're not allowed to ride in the ambulance.

Why don't you get dressed and have someone drive you? You'll be able to see your father at the hospital."

C. J. started to argue but saw the pleading look in her father's eyes. The paramedic gave her the hospital location, and the ambulance pulled away. Cursing to herself, she ran to get her car keys before she remembered her car was still at the police substation. With growing frustration she went to find the extra key to her father's car. As she ran down the stairs, she realized she was wearing nothing but her robe. She turned back to find something to wear.

At the hospital no one would tell her anything except that her father was stabilized and undergoing tests. Every time she reached the point of exploding, she would remember her father's voice chiding her not to be so harsh on people. She fought back tears and continued to pace the long hallway, trying to ignore the dozen or so people who also waited for word on a loved one. He had to be all right. She couldn't bear to lose him.

An hour later, her father's personal physician emerged. For an instant C. J. was struck by his resemblance to the tall, lanky Ichabod Crane character. He smiled and took her hand.

"Dr. Allen, how is he?" she demanded.

"C. J., I'm sorry you had to wait so long, but I wanted to be sure he was stabilized and out of danger before I spoke with you."

"What's happening?" Her stomach felt as if she had been eating lead.

"Your father had a mild heart attack. He's under a lot of stress right now, and with the hours he's working it just got to be too much."

"Stress? What stress?"

He looked at her with a small frown. "The business, of course. With everything that's been happening, he's exhausted."

C. J. started to comment but bit her tongue, embarrassed that her father's doctor knew more about the family business than she did. *They probably talked about the business when they played golf together*, she reasoned to herself. "Is he going to be okay?" she asked.

"With time and rest, he'll be fine. You'll have to help out more at the office, C. J. Take some of the burden off of him."

"I'll make him sell the damn business," she fumed.

Dr. Allen shook his head and took C. J.'s hand. "Now stop talking foolishness and listen to me. You and Riley Produce are what keeps your father going. He just has to realize he's not twenty-five anymore and slow down. I'm going to keep him here for as long as I can, but he's already ranting about going home. I want him to have bed rest for at least a week after I release him. Then you have to convince him to take a vacation. Assure him that you can hold everything together while he's gone. He trusts you. He needs at least a month, and three months would be even better. Can you do that?"

C. J. stared at the doctor in horror. "I couldn't run the business for an hour much less three months! He'd never leave me in charge."

He squeezed her hand more firmly and fixed her with a stern stare. "You either be prepared to take some of the burden off of your father or go home and plan his funeral. If he doesn't slow down, he's going to kill himself. Do you understand me?" His gaze captured and held hers. "You've played long enough, C. J. It's time to grow up and take some responsibility."

Tears burned her eyes as his words tore through her. She knew her father would never trust her with the business. Even if he did, she wouldn't be able to handle it.

"Don't worry." The doctor eased the grip on her hand and smiled. "Your father is always telling me how great you are. Now is the time to prove it. Dry your eyes and go in to see him. You can stay for five minutes. I've given him a sedative and ordered complete rest, so you won't be able to see him again today. Tomorrow morning you be here at ten sharp and be prepared to convince him that you can run Riley Produce for three months just as efficiently as he does." He smiled again and patted her hand. "Go on now."

With her heart in her throat, C. J. tiptoed into the intensive care unit. Her father's eyes were closed, and a heart monitor emitted ominous beeps. For an instant she panicked and was about to turn to flee when his eyes opened and stared at her. A slight smile crossed his lips. He motioned her in with his fingers. She approached the bed as if it were a guillotine. She took his hand. He gave hers a light squeeze. "I'll be fine," he said in a voice little more than a whisper. "Doc Allen has already said I can go home in a day or two."

"That's great." The words came out as a croak. The lump in her throat was choking her.

"Don't worry, honey. I'll be back home in no time."

C. J.'s mother had said the exact words to her on

the day she had left for the hospital. C. J. had been told it was a minor operation, but a brain tumor wasn't minor, and her mother hadn't come home.

In a fit of panic, C. J. began to babble. "Dad, don't rush back. Take some time off and rest. Let Ray handle things for a while. He's been wanting to run Riley Produce ever since he started working there." Her father smiled. Ray Mason's ambitions were a private joke between them.

"You know placing Ray in charge is not an option for discussion," he replied. "A lot of things are happening now. I have to be there, to be on top of it, or we could lose everything."

"Don't exaggerate," C. J. said. "You've got more money than even I can spend. You're always telling me that."

He shook his head slightly. "Things change, C. J. Do you ever listen to the news? We're struggling to find enough produce to fill orders. Fruit and vegetable crops have taken a major beating for three years running now. The orange crop in Florida last year was almost a total loss. The flooding in California, freezes here in the valley, and . . ." He trailed off and squeezed her hand. "Don't worry. I'll take care of it." He blinked slowly. The sedative was beginning to take effect.

"No, Dad. You've got to rest," C. J. pleaded.

"I will, darling, but I can't stand by and watch everything I've worked so hard for fall apart. I have to make sure you'll be secure." He was drifting off to sleep.

A nurse wearing a cheerful yellow smock touched C. J.'s arm. "You'll have to leave now."

"Can't I stay if I'm quiet?"

The nurse smiled and shook her head. "Sorry. Doctor's orders. Go home. The desk has your number in case we need to contact you."

C. J. clung to his hand, afraid to release it.

The nurse patted C. J.'s arm. "Dr. Allen would not have left him if your father were still in danger. Go home and rest. There's nothing to worry about."

Reluctantly C. J. released his hand and left the room. She stopped by the desk to make sure that they did indeed have her phone number. Then she went home, where a very concerned Alice met her at the door.

"How's Mr. Riley?" Alice asked before C. J. could close the door.

"He's had a mild heart attack."

Alice's hand flew to her own chest as if she were suffering a similar fate.

"Dr. Allen said he needs to rest and to take things slow for a while," C. J. informed her.

Alice sighed. "Telling him to slow down will be like trying to convince the sun not to shine," Alice declared. She shook her head so vigorously her tight mop of curls swayed.

"We'll just have to find a way to make him slow down," C. J. insisted. She started upstairs to lie down. Midway up she stopped and turned back to Alice.

"I'm sorry I yelled about the dry cleaning," she said before continuing up the stairs. She could feel Alice's astonished gaze follow her.

After an hour of tossing and turning, she got up and took a long hot shower, careful to avoid letting the water hit the still tender knot on her head. She dressed and went down to her father's study.

She sat at his desk and closed her eyes. She could smell the sharp scent of his cologne.

Alice popped her head in. "I promised to work a shift down at the children's clinic. I had already cleared it with Mr. Riley, but if you'd like I could call and cancel."

C. J. shook her head. "No, go ahead. I'll be fine."

"There's ham in the fridge if you'd like a sandwich, and I've left you a salad."

"I'm fine," C. J. assured her. She doubted her stomach would have been able to keep anything down.

After Alice left, C. J. stared out the window. Dr. Allen's warning played over and over again in her mind. How would she ever convince her father to slow down?

The hall clock struck five; the entire day had passed without her realizing it. Leaning forward she rested her aching head on her arms. The phone on the desk rang sharply, and C. J. stared until it rang a second time. She grabbed the receiver, praying it wasn't the hospital.

"Hello."

"C. J.?"

"Yes."

"It's Lois Franklin." C. J. breathed a sigh of relief. "I noticed your car was still here, and I was worried," Lois continued. "I mean, I was concerned that maybe you had gotten worse during the night. Are you all right?"

"Yeah." C. J. held her breath as her stomach did a series of somersaults at the sound of Lois's voice. "I just forgot to pick it up."

"Forgot." Lois paused. "You forgot to pick up a Jaguar V12?"

"My father had a mild heart attack this morning. I've been at the hospital all day."

"God, C. J., I'm sorry. I had no idea. Is he all right? Is there anything I can do?"

C. J. felt a warm rush from the concern in Lois's voice. "No, thanks. I'll have someone drive me down tomorrow for the car, if that's okay."

"Sure. It should be safe parked here," Lois said. She hesitated. "Listen, if you'd like, I could swing by your place and drive you over to pick it up. I mean, I do feel somewhat responsible."

C. J. suddenly wanted very much to see Lois. "Actually, that would be great if you don't mind. I hate driving my father's. It's one of those little short jobs, and I always feel like I'm a hood ornament."

"I could be there by six-thirty if that's convenient."

"That's fine. Thanks."

"See you then."

"Lois, wait," C. J. called out.

"Yeah?"

"I'm sorry for the way I acted last night and for what I said to you at Anne's. If I embarrassed you in front of my father I apologize. There are so many things." C. J. took a deep breath before continuing. "I guess I should just apologize for the entire evening," C. J. said, feeling miserable.

Lois was silent so long that C. J. almost asked if she was still there.

"I accept your apology," Lois started, "but you didn't embarrass me with your father. I just have to be careful. I can lose my job if they discover I'm a lesbian."

"Why?"

"Texas still has a sodomy law."

"What's that got to do with you? Isn't that a law against guys?"

"No. It applies to women also."

Lois carefully explained the sodomy law to her and how it could affect her job.

C. J. sat for a long while after Lois hung up and thought about how it must feel to fear losing your job. She had never faced discrimination due to her sexual orientation and didn't know anyone who had. It sounded like some archaic law, but apparently it still thrived. She rubbed her hands roughly over her face. It suddenly seemed like her ignorance had no bounds.

C. J. climbed into the truck and pulled the door closed. The sharp smell met her once more. A small koala bear hanging from the rearview mirror solved the mystery scent — eucalyptus. Her heart was pounding an irregular tune as she tried to think of something to say, something that wouldn't set both of them off again. "I would never have pictured you with a truck like this," she said, surprised to hear her voice sound so normal.

"What did you expect?" Lois asked as she pulled out of the driveway. She was wearing the reflective shades, and C. J. longed to ask her to remove them so she could see her eyes.

"I don't know. A little yellow Honda or something like that."

Lois's laugh was rich and smooth. C. J. wished she could make it go on forever. "That's what my father would call a responsible person's car," Lois informed her.

"I can't imagine you ever being anything other than responsible."

"Well, it just goes to show you how much you know about me."

"I would honestly like to know more," C. J. ventured nervously. Why had she said that? Now they would start in on each other again.

The perpetual frown returned to Franklin's face. "You don't give up, do you Riley? What exactly is it with you?"

C. J. took a deep breath. Maybe she should just lay her cards on the table. Why not go all the way in making a complete fool of herself? "I think I may be falling in love with you, or at least getting close to it," C. J. blurted.

Lois's gaze locked with hers for a second. "That's not funny, C. J."

"I didn't mean for it to be. I'm telling you the truth." If her clanging heart didn't slow down, she would soon be in intensive care with her father.

"How many times have you been in love?" Lois asked.

C. J. struggled to control her breathing. Why had she been stupid enough to start this conversation? Louis would think she was a total idiot. Besides, what did she know about love? This conversation had gotten too serious. She needed to lighten the mood. Her feelings for Lois were different from anything she had felt before, but was it love?

"I asked you a question," Lois reminded her.

Unable to look at her, C. J. turned her attention to the passing scenery. "Never. I've been in lust dozens of times." In an attempt at levity, she added, "I had a terrible crush on my fourth grade teacher. She didn't take me seriously either."

"It's hard to take you seriously," Lois said.

C. J. mentally kicked herself for being flippant at exactly the wrong time. Now Lois would never believe she was serious. *Are you serious?* a small voice nagged at her.

"What would I have to do to prove I'm serious?" she asked, hearing the faint tremble in her voice. She hoped Lois hadn't heard it as well.

"You couldn't handle it."

"Try me," C. J. challenged as she forced herself to turn to face Lois.

They stopped for a red light. Lois down shifted and glanced at her.

"Okay. First, you'd have to grow up. Second, you'd have to learn to take responsibility for your actions. And third, you'd have to learn that the world doesn't revolve around C. J. Riley."

The light changed, and they both fell silent as Lois went through the ritual of changing gears.

C. J. turned to stare out the window again. "There sure seems to be a sudden move toward making me take responsibility."

"What do you mean?" Lois asked.

C. J. related the warning the doctor had given her. "So, take over for a while and give your father a break," Lois encouraged. "You can handle it for three months. Or turn it over to someone else who works for your father. There's bound to be someone who can run the business." Lois added with a chuckle, "My mother says the secretary could run a business. But then she's a secretary, so she might be slightly biased."

C. J. shrugged and studied the toes of her sneakers. "I wouldn't even know where to begin. Not that it matters. He would never agree to turn it over to me or to anyone else."

As Lois took the exit ramp, C. J. wished she could slow the truck down. They would soon be at the police substation, and she didn't want their time together to end.

Lois glanced at her. "I thought you worked with your father. You said so the first day I stopped you."

C. J.'s stomach did a new series of somersaults. "You remember that."

Lois seemed to concentrate much harder on driving. "You made such a big deal about it. How could I forget?"

C. J. sat in silent thought. They were at the exit for the station. A feeling of desperation like none she had ever before experienced seized C. J. She had to find a way to convince Lois that she could change if Lois would give her some indication that she had a chance.

"Lois, could you ever be the least bit interested in me?" C. J. felt her body began to tremble as Lois pulled into the parking lot behind C. J.'s car.

"Leave it alone, C. J."

"I'm serious. Could you?"

Lois ran her hands through her hair. "Why are you

doing this? You only want me because I'm not falling all over myself to get to you. If I ever gave in, I wouldn't hold the least bit of interest to you."

She turned the truck ignition off and stared out the side window. Her voice dropped. "I've been through that once. I'll never do it again." She turned her intense gaze on C. J. "The next woman I fall in love with will have to be ready for a commitment, not just a casual fling. I'm tired of one-night stands."

Lois suddenly started the truck. She shook her head and turned to face C. J. "And, I don't think you're ready for that kind of commitment."

"If I was?" C. J. persisted and stared into her eyes.

Lois held her gaze and gave a small crooked smile. C. J.'s heart skipped a beat before Lois shook her head. "You'd never be happy. You like being irresponsible too much. It's in your blood."

C. J. stared out the window in forlorn silence. Her shoulders fell. Why couldn't she make Lois understand that nothing like this had ever happened to her before? "I've never had to take responsibility for anything," she tried to explain. "Dad has always taken care of everything." She shook her head and gave a self-depreciating chuckle. "I've never even balanced a checkbook."

"Poor little rich girl," Lois interjected with thick sarcasm.

"What the hell do you know?" C. J. shot back. Damn, she hadn't intended to let Lois get to her.

Lois sighed. "I know that as long as you sit there feeling sorry for yourself nothing will ever get done or change. If you want people to take you seriously, you're going to have to start taking yourself seriously."

"I want you to take me seriously." C. J. couldn't

look at her. She couldn't stand to see Lois mocking her.

"Then show me you can change."

C. J.'s head snapped toward Lois. "Does that mean . . . ?"

Lois held up her hand and stopped her. "It means we might eventually be friends, but I have to be honest with you." Her gaze held C. J. "I'd never allow myself to become involved with someone as irresponsible as you are."

Friends. C. J. ran the word around in her thoughts. Given time, friends could easily become lovers. C. J. felt as if she were standing on the edge of a great precipice. The right move would settle her onto safe ground—and the wrong one would send her tumbling beyond any chance of help. It was up to her to prove to Lois she could change.

C. J. squared her shoulders as she made her decision. For the first time in her life, she had a chance to make a difference. Actually, she was being given two chances—one, to make her father proud of her, and two, to win the respect of the woman she was falling in love with.

"Officer Lois Franklin, don't count Candice Jane Riley out of the running."

"Candice Jane!" Lois sputtered.

"That's right." C. J. opened the door and hopped to the ground, ignoring the small ripple of pain in her head. Hitching up her jeans and turning on her best smile, she looked up at Lois. "I'm officially declaring my intentions, Officer Franklin, so be thinking about where you want the wedding and who we should invite." She pulled the keys from her pocket as Lois shook her head, a slight smile tugging at the corners of her mouth.

C. J. continued. "But remember to make it on the weekend. We working stiffs have to schedule our time wisely." With a wink she shut the truck door and raced to her Jag. She had a lot to do and very little time in which to do it.

"How is Mr. Riley?" Janice demanded the minute she heard C. J.'s voice on the phone. C. J. wondered vaguely how Janice knew and then felt guilty that she hadn't thought to call her. Alice had probably called her. C. J. had called Janice after she got home from picking up her Jag.

"Dr. Allen says he will be fine," C. J. explained. "But he's going to have to take it easier. Dr. Allen wants Dad to take three months off."

"Oh, dear," Janice declared. "He'll never do that. But I can make sure that some of the pressure is taken off of him here. The other members of the board will simply have to start doing more."

"What about Ray?" C. J. asked, knowing her dad would never agree to leaving him in control, but she needed to see how Janice felt.

"Never," she replied quickly. "Ray is too strung out over his divorce. He barely does his own job." She stopped suddenly as if remembering who she was talking too.

C. J.'s palms were sweating. "Janice, I need your help."

"Anything," Janice answered without hesitation.

"I want to take over for Dad for three months. I have to convince him I'll be able to do it. Will you help me?"

C. J. held her breath as the silence between them grew. "Janice, please," she begged. "I have to do this, and I can't without your help."

"C. J., running Riley Produce is a little more complicated than me just slipping you a few notes to review. I can't run this place," Janice said.

"I'm not asking you to," C. J. explained. "Just help me get well enough acquainted with what's going on so I can convince Dad to let me try." She took a deep breath and let it out slowly. "Once I'm there, the board will help me."

When Janice didn't respond C. J. tried again.

"Janice, I know the other board members don't like me and everyone thinks I'm a total screwup, but they won't let Dad down. They will work with me to help him." C. J. could sense she wasn't winning. In frustration she grabbed her head and yelled. "Damn it, Janice. I don't want him to die."

"What do you want me to do?" Janice asked at last.

C. J. took another deep breath to calm herself. "Meet me at the office as soon as you can," C. J. said.

"I'll be there in twenty minutes, and you'd better be there when I arrive," Janice said in a voice that left no doubt that she meant it.

C. J. shouted to Alice to let her know where she would be and ran from the house. She was sitting in a chair by Janice's desk when Janice walked in promptly twenty minutes after their conversation.

Janice Greeley appeared to be in her late fifties or early sixties. She had been C. J.'s father's secretary for as long as C. J. could remember. Janice always dressed in tailored jackets and skirts. Her short, almost completely white hair fell into clumps of curls around her soft face. C. J. knew little of her personal life, only that there was a husband who had retired after twenty-five years of driving a truck for Riley Produce and that her father thought highly of Janice, which was all the recommendation C. J. needed.

"Let's get started," Janice said without preamble. "We will start with our customer base. You should be a little familiar with that. Then we'll cover buyer and seller records, produce reports, and market studies. After that, if you're still interested, we'll take a run through the accounts."

Janice gave her a long look, and C. J. realized that Janice thought this was a waste of her time. *Well, I'll show everybody that C. J. Riley can be as responsible as anyone else*, she thought and pulled the chair closer to Janice's desk.

It was seven-thirty the next morning when C. J. returned home to shower and change. She and Janice had spent the entire night reviewing the items that Janice felt C. J. should know. Janice spent hours filling C. J. in on the business events that had shaped C. J.'s father's world during the last few years. Events that C. J. had never found interesting suddenly took on new meaning. She found she could grasp the information easily once she decided to listen. She now felt armed with enough information to convince her father to let her try.

* * * * *

Mr. Riley had been moved to a private room. He was awake and staring at a muted TV when C. J. entered the room. He was still pale, but his skin was losing its sickly gray tone. C. J. forced herself to ignore the machines that were still wired to his body and to concentrate on the sweet aroma of the flowers that barely concealed the irritating hospital smells. She kissed him on the cheek and took a deep breath.

"Dad, we need to talk."

He glanced at her with a surprised look on his face. "Sounds serious. What's up?" he asked.

"I had a long talk with Dr. Allen yesterday."

"If Ivan said anything to upset you . . ."

"Listen to me," she insisted. "He did upset me, but he also made me think. The truth is, I've always been afraid of Riley Produce," she blurted out.

"C. J. —"

She held up her hand. "Please let me finish. Riley Produce has always been this huge indefinable being to me. I could never understand it. The whole thing intimidated me. But more than that, I never had any reason to have to understand it. Yesterday, Dr. Allen told me that if you didn't slow down you could die."

"I'll talk to him." He closed his eyes and sighed. "I'm sorry he frightened you. I'm fine. I'll be up and around before —"

"Dad! You're not listening to me!"

He opened his eyes to gaze at her. Unable to meet his stare, she began pacing beside the bed. "There's something else." She stopped and stared intently at him. How was she ever going to convince him to slow down? *Don't let him see how scared you are*, she told herself. *Look him in the eye and tell him the truth.* "I think I've met the woman that I want to spend the rest of my life with." Her words shocked her almost as much as they did him. She had intended to say something about him resting.

C. J. felt a stab of guilt when she saw the relief reflected in his eyes. "I'm glad," he said quietly. "C. J., you know I don't understand your lifestyle and it has always concerned me that you've never seemed particularly happy. But if you could meet, excuse me," he corrected, "*have* met a woman who will make you happy, then I'm pleased for you."

C. J. blinked back her tears. "There's a catch. She can't stand me."

He ran a hand through his hair. C. J.'s attention focused on the long tube that trailed from his arm.

"Is this the woman who sent the earrings back?"

C. J. felt her face burn with embarrassment. "No, that was someone else." *How can anyone take me seriously?* she wondered.

Mr. Riley hesitated. "Honey, I'm sorry, but I don't know what to say." He began to turn the edge of the sheet into an accordionlike fold.

C. J. tried to explain. "She says I have to learn to be more responsible, and she's right." She tactfully ignored her father's head nodding in agreement. "Dad, I need your help. You have to turn Riley Produce over to me completely for three months."

He stared at her in total disbelief. "C. J., no! I'll gladly give you more responsibility, but not a full take-over."

"No. I want complete control for three months.

You've wanted me to be more involved in Riley Produce and now is the time to let me prove that I can do it."

"C. J., be reasonable. You're talking about a multimillion-dollar business here. A business that is facing some serious setbacks."

"I know. I've been studying the accounts and going over the books all night," she assured him as she pulled a chair next to the bed and took his hand. "I think I can do it. You've got to give me a chance." She could see the doubt in his eyes. "I have a couple of ideas about how we could obtain enough produce to fill orders. We could buy crops from small farmers. I know they can be harder to deal with because the buyer does the same amount of work for smaller volumes and it may cost us a little more, but we'd still make a profit and we'd be filling orders. Let me try, Dad."

"No," he said, giving his head an adamant shake.

"What's the worst that can happen?" C. J. leaned toward him on the edge of her chair.

He looked at her, shocked.

C. J. tried to lighten the mood and flashed her best smile. "The worse thing would be that I'd lose every penny you ever made and then I'd have to go out and find a job like everyone else."

He shook his head. "C. J., this isn't a joke. And don't think that smile of yours is going to win me over on this," he said, pointing his finger at her. She nodded and sat quietly. A long silence fell between them, while he studied her.

"You say you've gone over the accounts and you

think you're prepared. Tell me exactly what you would do on Monday morning if I were to turn everything over to you."

She fidgeted in her chair. "Damn, what is this? A quiz?"

"You want Riley Produce. You have exactly thirty minutes to convince me you can handle it."

C. J. could see the challenge in his eyes. *He's enjoying this*, she realized. *All right*, she thought, *the ball is in my court and I'll play your game.*

"The first thing I'd do is call a staff meeting to inform the board of the temporary changes. Then I'd ask each of the VPs to get me their status reports for Tuesday's meeting. I'd check with Mary to see how the new campaign for Texas apples is coming along . . ."

She spent the next thirty minutes answering the multitude of questions he fired at her and responding to his inquiries on how she would handle this or that situation should it arise. When it looked as though he had her cornered on something, she would change tactics and charge from another angle. More than once she sent a silent thank-you to Janice.

At last, he leaned back against his pillow, and she could see he was wavering. She moved from the chair to the edge of his bed and took his hand.

"I need for you to be able to depend on me now," C. J. said in a voice thickened with honest emotion. "Don't you see? I've never had anyone need me for anything."

"Honey, I've always needed you."

She left the bed and resumed her pacing, her arms

waving. "You've always needed me to be your little girl. I need more now. Dad, I have to prove to myself that I can do this. I have to prove it to Lois."

"Officer Franklin?" he asked with raised eyebrows. "You're in love with Officer Franklin?"

"What's wrong with that?" C. J. bristled, hands on hips.

He stared at her for a second before shaking his head. "Nothing."

"Dad, don't you see? If you can't trust me to be responsible, how can anyone else? You said yesterday that you wanted to be sure I was secure. Well, now is the time to see if I can make it on my own." She dug her nails into her palms to stop the tears that were burning the backs of her eyes. "Please give me this chance."

He sat quietly for a moment, staring at her, and then cleared his throat. "I've been wanting to go to Denver to visit my brother, Martin. From there I think maybe I'll go to Florida for some deep-sea fishing. I don't want anyone to think they can count on me to bail you out if you hit a rough spot." C. J. held her breath as he continued. "I'll call my lawyer and have the necessary paperwork drawn up. You'll be in complete charge. You've got three months to prove yourself."

C. J. felt her knees go weak. He was really going to do it. She would be in charge of Riley Produce! Somehow she managed to make it to the bed to hug him. He chuckled and patted her shoulder as she fought back tears of joy and fright. "I know you won't let me down," he said.

Dr. Allen arrived at that moment to tell them that Mr. Riley could be released the following day if everything continued well. While her father was busy telling him about C. J. taking over Riley Produce and his extended vacation, C. J. eased out of the room and raced down the hall to the rest room, where she was promptly sick.

C. J. parked her car in a visitor's slot at Anne's apartment complex. She felt in her pocket for the letter she had written. She was sure Anne wouldn't see her, so she had come prepared to leave the letter.

She approached the apartment with a deep sense of shame and rang the door bell. Taking the letter from her pocket, she knelt to slip it under the door. It swung open. Anne, her long black hair hanging loose down her back, looked down. She was dressed in a pair of tan slacks and a brown sweater.

"Getting on your knees won't help at this point, C. J." Anne folded her arms and leaned against the door frame. The circles under her eyes hurt C. J. more than any words she could have spoken.

"Anne." C. J. scrambled to her feet. "I, uh, I wanted to apologize for the other night." She reached into her pocket for the earrings. "You didn't have to return these. I'd like for you to keep them."

Anne pushed her hand away. "I thought you gave me things because you enjoyed it. I never knew you were buying me. It's too late. Good-bye."

"Wait," C. J. pleaded. Anne stopped. C. J. took a deep breath and slowly exhaled. "I didn't mean for it to be that way, and I know it's too late, but I still wanted to say I'm sorry. I had no right to say what I did to you. I was angry and took it out on you. I apologize." She slid the offensive earrings into her pocket.

"Fine, you've apologized." Anne stepped back to close the door.

C. J. grabbed it before it could close. "Look, I know I've been a total ass, but could we just talk for a minute?"

Anne stared at her through the small opening. "I'm not taking you back."

"I understand, but I'd really like to talk to you."

"About what?" The pain in her eyes was too much for C. J. She dropped her gaze to the letter in her hand and shrugged. What did she want? To tell Anne that she was becoming responsible? To say that she needed to share her excitement and fear at this new turn in her life with someone? Anne stared at her with eyes devoid of any warmth.

"C. J., I have nothing left to say to you, so please leave."

C. J. knew she had no right to be here, not after the horrible things she had said. She stepped away from the door as it closed and the lock fell into place. She walked back to her car. After several minutes of staring into space, she drove to a nearby post office and mailed the letter. Maybe it would convince Anne she was truly sorry. C. J. wished there was some way she could erase the pain she saw in her eyes.

Guiltily she ran back through her life, reviewing it. There was very little that she could feel proud of. She had spent her life thinking of no one but herself. Somehow, she promised herself, she would change. She would make her life mean something to someone other than herself. Would that be enough for Lois?

She drove by the jewelry store to return the

earrings. The woman met her with a sultry smile. "Coming back to check out the merchandise again?"

"I need to return these. The receipt's inside the box," C. J. said quickly.

The woman stared at the box with raised eyebrows. "Felix," she called over her shoulder, never taking her eyes off C. J. She handed him the box and told him to take care of it.

"Why don't you come on back with me," she whispered.

C. J. stared at the woman and realized she didn't even know her name. How many women had she been with? How many faces had she forgotten? For the first time since she had come out, she stood facing an extremely attractive, hot woman and didn't feel the slightest urge to have sex with her. "Another time, maybe," she said as she left.

CHAPTER FOUR

On Monday morning C. J. was sitting at her father's desk by five-thirty. At promptly six-forty-five Janice arrived. The surprised look on her face told C. J. that her appearance would indeed be a shock to everyone.

C. J. picked up a stack of papers and headed for Janice's desk. "I need this mailed." She handed her an envelope that held the two traffic citations and a check. "And I'll need to see these files," she said, and handed her a list of names. "I also want a meeting of the board at eight o'clock. Would you make sure this letter goes out to all of the employees?" C. J. handed her more papers. Janice made notes on a pad. C. J. hesitated before adding, "You'd better hold the letter to the employees until after the board meeting."

"Dropping a surprise on them, are we?" Janice said with a laugh. Her brown eyes sparkled with pleasure at being included in the conspiracy.

"They're not going to be very happy," C. J. acknowledged. "I know what they think of me." She looked around, uncomfortable with the thought. "The truth is, they're right. I've never taken anything seriously in my life. I hope I don't let my father down."

Janice patted her hand. "I've worked for your father for twenty-four years. He would never allow anything to endanger Riley Produce. There are too many people who depend on him for jobs."

C. J. felt the strength drain from her body as she collapsed into the chair beside Janice's desk. "God, I'm still doing it," she whispered.

"C. J.," Janice said, as she hovered. "Are you okay? You're white as a sheet."

C. J. dropped her head into her hands and rested her elbows against her knees. "I'm still thinking only of myself," she muttered. "It never occurred to me that if I screwed this up, people other than me will suffer." She jumped up, almost knocking an astonished Janice down. "I can't do this," she said in a panic. "I have to call my father and tell him I've changed my mind." She moved toward the phone.

"C. J. Riley," Janice snapped, her eyes blazing. "I'll not hear of you disturbing your father. He has worked himself sick for you, to give you everything you've wanted. Do you have any idea how much that car you

71

drive cost? That was an entire lemon crop. Now, you're going to stiffen up that Riley backbone of yours and face this the way your father would. Furthermore —"

C. J.'s laughter bubbled over.

Janice glared at her as though she had lost her mind. "I see nothing amusing."

"I'm sorry, Janice," C. J. said, wiping the tears from her eyes. "I was just thinking that the Jag's manufacturer would probably faint if they heard the word *lemon* used in the same sentence as their car."

Janice relaxed and straightened her almond-colored jacket. "Well, yes, I can see where that may not have been the right description of payment."

In a rare display of affection, C. J. hugged her. "It was exactly right, and so were you. I won't let him down," she promised, stepping back away from her.

"Good," Janice said and nodded as she picked up her notepad. "Now what else needs to be done before we allow the lions into the den?"

C. J. entered the small conference room clutching a file folder. Her palms were sweating so badly the folder was damp. She had never let other people's opinions of her bother her, but suddenly it was very important that these four board members grow to respect her. Without their help she would not be able to pull this off. She gazed at them. *I can do this*, she reassured herself.

As she approached, Ray Mason's well-muscled body stood and moved to the side of the table where he pulled out a chair for her. He had been sitting in her father's place.

Ray was vice president, purchasing, and it was common knowledge that he had high hopes of someday running Riley Produce. What he didn't know was that her father had no intentions of ever letting him run the company. Ray was the son of her father's best friend, Ralph Mason. Ray had been fired from numerous jobs before Ralph begged Carlton to hire him. To Ray's credit he had settled down, worked steady, and had honestly achieved his promotions.

Things had gone well for him until his wife, Sue, divorced him a few months earlier. He had been so distraught over the divorce that he started drinking and missing work. He began causing problems within his department. Her father had finally insisted that Ray take a few weeks off. Ray seemed to be doing much better after returning.

"C. J.," he said, as she walked across the room. "We were all upset to hear about your father, but don't worry. Everything is under control."

C. J. knew she was probably about to make a powerful enemy, but she had to establish her authority right away. "I appreciate everyone's concern," she said. Instead of continuing on around the table, she stopped at the head where Ray's notebook was laid out. With her heart pounding in her ears, she folded his notebook and slid it toward the chair he was holding for her. She heard someone gasp as she sat in her father's chair.

"We have a lot to get through this morning, so why don't we get started?" Her gaze locked with Ray's. His face was mottled, and she could see beads of sweat starting to glow on his forehead. He looked away and stood staring down at the table, gripping the chair back. She swallowed, praying that her voice would not betray her fear.

"Janice, would you pass out the agenda and we'll get —"

"C. J.," Ray cut in, his voice shaking in anger. "You can't seriously be thinking about trying to run Riley Produce."

C. J. looked around the table at the rest of the board. Grover Clayton, vice president, sales, sat leaning back in his chair, his generous stomach overlapping his belt. Hank Holbrook, vice president, operations, was a small nervous man who constantly pulled at his thin, graying mustache. They were both smiling their encouragement at Ray. Mary Acosta, vice president, advertising, the final board member, was staring at her. Mary was a pretty woman with smooth caramel skin and deep brown eyes that were framed by long, thick dark lashes. C. J.'s rapidly slipping confidence was reinforced when Mary gave her a slight nod of support. It was so quick and subtle C. J. would wonder later if it had even happened. She looked toward Janice and received a brief encouraging smile. C. J. took a deep breath.

"Perhaps you can give me a reason why I shouldn't." She wished she hadn't sat down. He was still standing and seemed twice as intimidating.

"You're not qualified," he answered with bold assurance.

His bluntness only widened the slice of self-doubt she was experiencing. A vision of her father lying in intensive care came to her. She had to succeed.

"What do you base your assumption on?" she asked, leaning back in the chair and meeting his glare with what she hoped was a neutral expression.

He looked to Grover and Hank for support and apparently received it, because he drew himself up to his full impressive height of six feet two inches and sneered. "This is a business, not a party room for lesbians." Grover snickered.

C. J. silenced Grover's amusement with a glare. She felt as though Ray's words had struck her physically. How had this gone from her business abilities to her sexuality? Never in her previous encounters with these people had her sexuality been mentioned.

She forced herself to look back at Ray and hold his gaze as she calmly took the time to lean forward and place her folded hands on the table. How would her father handle this? That was an easy one — Carlton Riley would have fired him on the spot. C. J. knew she didn't have that luxury. She would need everyone's knowledge to pull this off.

"Ray," she said, forcing a smile, "I'll make a deal with you. You keep your personal opinions out of the boardroom and I'll keep my women out of it."

She turned away from his anger and directed her attention to the papers Janice was distributing. "There's a copy of today's agenda. I also have a list of reports I'll need from each of you for tomorrow's regular meeting."

"You aren't listening," Ray said, his voice low and shaking with anger. "We aren't going to allow you to do this." He gathered up the papers Janice was distributing and flung them back at C. J. "I'll be in charge until Carlton can return. I'm sure that's what he would want." He straightened his tie. "You can continue on with whatever it is you do."

C. J. forced herself not to grab his tie and strangle him. Instead she took a deep breath and pulled the paper she had hoped she wouldn't need from the file folder in front of her.

"This is a power of attorney, signed by my father giving me —" Ray lunged across the table and snatched the paper from her hand. Grover and Hank were on their feet, faces red, eyes bulging. Mary Acosta spun her gold pen on the table. Janice was smiling and making doodles on her notepad, while Ray frantically read the paper.

"As I was saying," C. J. continued, "my father has given me complete control over Riley Produce for the next three months. So if everyone will please sit down, we'll continue with the meeting."

"He can't do this," Ray hissed. "I'm supposed to take charge. You never did anything here. What right do you have?" His eyes smoldered with visible hatred as he approached her. She was afraid to stand, scared it would trigger an attack, and was just as afraid to remain seated. The depth of his emotions startled her.

"Ray, sit down!" Mary Acosta snapped. "I have work to do, and it won't get done if I have to sit in here listening to you whine all day. May I have a copy of an agenda please?" She held out her hand.

Janice appeared and took the papers from C. J. They were again distributed to each member. A neat stack was placed by Ray's notebook. He was still standing beside C. J., glaring at her.

Ignore him, she told herself. *Go on with the*

meeting. She opened her mouth to speak, but once again Ray stopped her.

"I'll quit," he growled.

C. J.'s stomach dropped. This she feared more than physical confrontation, but this had to stop. If she was going to succeed she had to have the respect of the officers.

"Ray," she said, standing to look up at him. "I would truly be sorry to see you go. You're a valuable asset to Riley Produce; however, I intend to run this company to the best of my ability for at least the next three months. I would be grateful for your help and support, but if you can't accept that, then I'll respect your decision to quit."

The room was deathly quiet. Ray looked to Grover and Hank for support, but they were both engrossed with studying their agendas. He stormed from the boardroom, and C. J. felt her chance of success diminish with his departure.

Somehow the day went by. Janice had been close at hand all day to explain things C. J. didn't understand. Hank and Grover had slipped in separately to tell her how happy they were that she was taking over instead of Ray. They each gave her a lengthy rundown on their many and greatly needed responsibilities. C. J. had spoken to her father. He had been released from the hospital and Ivan Allen, his doctor, was taking him home to rest. True to his word, her father never mentioned Riley Produce. She didn't have the heart or nerve to tell him Ray had quit.

*   *   *   *   *

Janice came in at six to tell her she was leaving for the day. C. J. thanked her again for her help and waved good-bye. Another hour slipped away while C. J. finished reading and signing the last of the correspondence on her desk. The building had settled into a comfortable silence.

The phone rang and shattered the silence. Wondering who would be calling this late, she answered it. There was no one there, but she could tell the line was still open.

"Hello," she said again. There was still no response, so she hung up. *Must be a wrong number*, she reasoned.

C. J. poured herself a drink from the small wet bar, kicked off her flats, and propped up her feet on the huge mahogany desk. The bourbon burned a path down her throat. Setting the glass aside, she rubbed her tired eyes. They felt like sandpaper had been glued to the lids. There was a dull ache in her temples. Whether it was from the stress of the day or from Saturday's fall, she wasn't sure. Slowly she let herself relax and think about Lois Franklin.

A hand closed around her leg. C. J. managed to stifle the full-blown scream that rose in her throat to a mere yelp.

Mary Acosta stepped back surprised. "I didn't mean to scare you, but sleeping in the office is a bad habit to start. You never know when the boss will walk through and catch you," she teased. A mischievous sparkle filled her eyes.

C. J. put her feet on the floor and gasped at the pinpoints of pain that filled her blood-starved legs. "I guess feet propping is another managerial skill I need to be working on," she said and grinned.

"I came by to congratulate you on how you handled things today." Mary said, running her hand under her shoulder-length hair and pushing it away from her neck.

"I lost the company's leading buyer. What do I tell our customers next month when we don't have enough produce to fill orders?" C. J. asked, massaging her legs through her woolen slacks. As she bent over, she noticed Mary's shapely legs. For a brief moment she let herself speculate on what it would feel like to run her hand slowly up them.

Mary's voice snapped her out of her daydreaming. "He never actually did the bulk of the purchasing. You'll just have to do twice the amount of managing until you can replace him." Mary flashed a dazzling smile that displayed a lifetime of excellent dental care.

C. J. groaned. "That's just what I need."

Mary sat down in a chair in front of the huge desk. "You know your father has been the major buyer for the company all along. The truth is, over the past year Ray has become almost as big a token as . . ." She trailed off, embarrassed.

C. J. let the slip go by. She knew Mary had almost commented on C. J.'s token position. She spoke quickly to help cover Mary's embarrassment. "I know Dad was always out of town looking over potential crops." She continued to rub life back into her aching legs.

"You could do the same thing," Mary suggested.

C. J. stared in amazement. "What do I know about fruits and vegetables?"

Mary laughed and shook her head. A moment of

silence fell between them. Mary gave a nervous cough. "I actually stayed late for a reason," she began. "I was wondering . . ." She stood up and began to pace the length of the desk and back before coming to a halt in front of C. J. "I'd like the VP, purchasing, position. I'm good with people, and I'd like to be on the buying end of the business rather than the selling. I want to work the job as it was intended to be."

C. J. sat back in the chair and listened.

"I've been the head of advertising for seven years," Mary continued. "I know our customers and what they're looking for better than anyone. I think I can take that knowledge out to the growers and help pick the best produce for the business." She raised her hand as if to stop the still silent C. J. and began pacing again. "I know what you're thinking. I don't have experience in buying. But I've studied the market reports, and I know what a fair price for the produce is." She stopped and leaned across the desk. Her eyes were sparkling. C. J. was struck by a sudden jealousy of her intense passion.

"C. J., I really want this job."

To buy some time, C. J. studied her nails. Giving Mary this job would throw two departments open for change. No one liked change. "Who would you recommend to fill your position?"

"Sylvia Longoria. She's been my manager of advertising for six years. She's good. Advertising won't even know I'm gone."

"Who will fill her position?"

"That's up to her. Each VP fills positions for their department. She'll pick the best qualified person." Mary was practically wringing her hands.

"Let me think a minute," C. J. said.

Mary sat down on the edge of her chair.

C. J. swiveled her chair to stare at the large seascape on the wall beside her. What would her father do? Slowly she weighed the pros and cons of moving Mary into the position before turning back around.

"I'll do it on one condition." She saw the suspicion in Mary's eyes. "You have to teach me everything you know about our customers." Mary jumped up, fists raised in a victory salute. "And," C. J. continued, "you let me go with you to meet the growers. At least until I get the hang of it."

Mary extended her hand. "You're on."

C. J. shook her hand and smiled. "Finally, I've made someone happy. Let me pour us a drink to celebrate." C. J. crossed to the bar and poured them each a drink. "Sorry. There's only bourbon," she said, offering Mary the glass.

"That's fine."

"Here's to Riley Produce's new vice president, purchasing, Mary Acosta," C. J. said as she raised her glass. They clinked their glasses and each took a sip.

"I'll have my secretary type up the necessary paperwork for Sylvia and get it to you for signature first thing tomorrow morning," Mary said, staring at the amber liquid in her glass.

"Is everything okay?" C. J. asked, noticing the pensive look on Mary's face.

"I was wondering if it would be appropriate for me to ask you to dinner?" Mary asked and gazed at her.

C. J. felt her pulse quicken. *She's straight*, she reminded herself. Recalling Ray's remark about her sexuality, she suddenly found herself in the uncomfortable position of wondering if Mary was referring to the appropriateness of asking a lesbian to dinner or asking her boss. Only one way to know for sure, she decided. "Are you referring to asking your boss or asking a lesbian to dinner?"

Mary said hesitantly, "In this case I suppose both apply."

Relieved, C. J. gave a nervous laugh. "Well, as your lesbian boss, let me assure you that both of those sterling qualities are starving. Where to? My treat."

"Lesson number one, C. J.," Mary said as she sat her glass down and headed for the door. "The person getting the new job buys. So dinner is on me."

"We seem to have a problem then," C. J. said, standing up to follow her.

Mary stopped and looked back at her, frowning. "How's that?"

"Today's my first day on a new job as well."

Mary shrugged, "Then it looks like it's Dutch treat."

CHAPTER FIVE

During the next three weeks C. J. worked as she had never dreamed of working in her life. She was up by four each morning, in the office by five, and rarely out before eight each evening. She fell into bed every night exhausted but with a new sense of satisfaction. Contracted orders were being filled on time, and new ones continued to flow in. Riley Produce had not yet fallen apart under her guidance.

The only thing that did seem unusual was that each day soon after Janice left, the phone would ring. When C. J. answered there was no sound other than someone breathing. After the first week, C. J. stopped answering it, but it continued to ring daily.

Her friend Ron had also been calling practically every day wanting her to play tennis or to go shopping. Each time C. J. explained that she was busy and couldn't go, but he refused to give up. She finally gave in and promised to go shopping with him on Saturday since James would be working.

She had thought of Lois often and had dialed her number several times, but she had hung up when the answering machine kicked in. C. J.'s father had left for his vacation, and he had called her once from Denver. He didn't mention Riley Produce.

C. J. met Ron in Rivercenter Mall at eleven Saturday morning. He was wanting to shop for his new summer wardrobe. She knew when she saw his face that he was in a foul mood. Before they reached the shop, he began complaining about having to fight the heavier weekend crowd.

"I don't know why you couldn't come with me on Thursday like I asked," he said with a pout.

"I told you. I had a board meeting and couldn't get away."

"You're starting to sound as boring as James." They were looking through a rack of men's shorts. A young saleswoman approached them.

"May I help you find something?"

"No, you may not!" Ron snapped.

The woman apologized and left.

"Why did you do that?" C. J. asked.

"What?"

"She was just trying to help you."

"Did I ask for her help?" He looked after the woman. "What would she know about fashion anyway? She looks like a bag lady."

"Ron, that's cruel. Besides," she said, slipping into their usual banter, "I haven't seen you on the cover of *GQ* lately."

He stared at her. "Go fuck yourself," he spat and stormed out of the store.

Shocked, C. J. called to him, but he kept going. She ran after him and caught up with him just before he reached his car.

"Ron, I'm sorry." She tried to put an arm around his shoulder, but he pushed her away.

"Leave me alone!"

C. J. realized he was crying. "Hey, I didn't mean to upset you. I was only teasing."

His sobs grew heavier. People around them were starting to stare. "Come on," C. J. insisted and took his arm. "Let's get out of here." She led him to his BMW and crawled in beside him. "What's wrong?"

"Everything is changing," he said, with a flood of fresh tears.

"What's changing?" she asked and held his hand.

"You're working and starting to sound more like James every day, and . . . and John's moving."

"Who's John?" she asked confused.

"The tennis pro I was telling you about. You met him the last time we played tennis. He's moving to San Francisco." He hesitated. "He's asked me to go with him."

"Leave James!"

Ron nodded and blew his nose on a tissue C. J. had found for him. Ron was the only real friend she had. What would she do if he left?

"Are you going to?" C. J. asked. She was almost afraid to hear his answer. What would James do?

"Of course not." He gave her a look that said he was doubting her sanity.

C. J. realized she had been holding her breath and exhaled loudly. "God, you scared me. I thought for a moment you'd fallen in love with this guy."

"I do love him!" he screamed and pounded his fist against the seat.

C. J. was at a loss. She wasn't sure how to handle his outbursts. "Do you still love James?" she asked tentatively.

He shrugged and stared out the window.

"Ron. You do love James, don't you?" They were the only "couple" she knew. In a strange way she had always envied their relationship and the security they must have in knowing someone would always be there no matter what.

He turned slowly to look at her. "I'll never leave James, if that's what you're worried about." New tears started. "It's just that I love John so much. I don't know why he can't stay here with me," he continued.

"Do you love him more than you love James?"

He nodded.

C. J. felt sick. "Then maybe you should go with John." She couldn't believe she had actually suggested that.

Ron stared at her again with that are-you-crazy look and said, "I could never live on what John makes!"

C. J. sat stunned as the implication of what he

was telling her began to sink in. She bit her tongue to keep from saying something she would regret. Then a reality she didn't want to face hit her.

She stared at him horrified as she realized they had always been so much alike. Money ruled their lives. Could she ever live without it? Would she be willing to give up everything if Lois were to ask her? Ron burst into a fresh wave of tears, and C. J. pulled him into her arms. As she held him while he cried, she realized there were things more important than money.

C. J. placed the second suitcase by her door; she had left the office early to pack. She and Mary were leaving for the valley the next morning to visit a group of small farms. The trip would be a first for them and Riley Produce. The company traditionally dealt with the major operations that could sell large volumes of produce.

As this was their first visit with the growers, they were both nervous, but Mary's confidence was getting C. J. through. Glancing at her watch, C. J. saw it was only a little after seven. Picking up the phone, she dialed Lois's number. Her heart nearly stopped when Lois answered on the second ring.

"Hello, Lois. C. J. Riley calling."

There was a brief silence. "C. J.?" She heard a sigh. "I don't suppose it would do me any good to ask how you got this number."

"I did give my word not to tell," C. J. said, and smiled into the receiver.

"I thought you had given up on me," Lois said.

"Never. I've been working. My father went on vacation, and I'm filling in."

"I'm proud of you," Lois said.

C. J. felt a warm glow. "I'm leaving tomorrow to visit some growers in the valley and I was wondering if you might consider going out to dinner with me tonight."

There was a brief pause. "I'm kind of busy."

"We could make it a short evening. I have to be up early to get to the airport."

Lois hesitated.

"Please." C. J. twirled the cord nervously around her finger. "Just as a friend."

There was another long pause before Lois spoke. "Okay. But understand, this is dinner. Nothing else."

C. J.'s heart leapt. "Dinner only. We'll sit on opposite sides of the table, get separate checks, and I promise I won't ask to taste anything on your plate."

Lois laughed a magical laugh that sent C. J.'s heart into a new biorhythm. They settled on a rib place that was located centrally between them.

Lois was at the table drinking a beer when C. J. arrived. Lois was wearing jeans and a work shirt over a dark blue tank top. She smiled and shook her head as C. J. started toward their table.

"At least you're prompt, Candice Jane."

C. J. winced at the name, but smiled to hide it. "I was afraid I was late when I saw you were here already," she admitted. She didn't tell Lois that she had changed clothes three times before finally giving up and grabbing her favorite jeans and pullover.

"No, I'm early. Would you like a beer?"

"Sure." C. J. found it hard not to stare into those clear blue eyes.

Lois flagged the waitress. The sleeves of her work shirt were rolled to her elbows. C. J. felt a light sweat break out on her back as she studied Lois's long, thin fingers and strong, well-defined forearms. She was imagining how those hands would feel when the waitress plopped her beer down and startled her.

C. J. and Lois made the usual small talk about the weather until the waitress took their meal orders.

"Tell me the story behind Candice Jane," Lois prompted.

There's not much to tell," C. J. stated. "My paternal grandmother was named Candice, and my maternal grandmother was named Jane."

"Must be a real burden for you," Lois said and gave a slight smile. Her tank top slipped just enough to show a hint of cleavage. Tearing her eyes away, C. J. busied herself by making impressions with her thumbnail on the napkin around her beer bottle.

"Not really. My family calls me C. J., and no one except you, outside my family, knows."

Lois sipped her beer. "Well, Candice Jane, I consider it a real honor to have been entrusted with such a secret. I'll guard it closely. I promise."

C. J. felt herself smiling like a fool.

Lois looked away suddenly and began to scratch at the label on her beer bottle. "How are you finding corporate life?" Lois asked, abandoning the label and resting her chin on the heel of her hand.

C. J. thought about mentioning the phone calls, but didn't want to sound paranoid. "It's a lot like playing tennis," C. J. said. She drew stick figures on her bottle by running her finger through the condensation. "You just have to concentrate on what you want to happen and hope you can pull it off before your opponent does. How's the ticket business?"

"Much slower now that you're off the road," Lois shot back with a smile. "How's your father?"

"When I heard from him last week, he was lying on some beach in Florida soaking up sunshine."

"It's a good thing you're doing, C. J.," Lois said. "Your father is lucky to have you here."

C. J.'s heart pounded. The food arrived and saved her from having to think of a response. They worked over the food faithfully for a few minutes.

"What about your family?" C. J. asked, wiping a smear of barbecue sauce from her hand.

"My father is an economics professor at Incarnate Word, and, as I mentioned, my mother is a secretary. She works for a group of architects downtown."

"Brothers or sisters?"

"Two each. All married and living in other cities." Lois took a drink of water.

"It must be great having a big family."

Lois shrugged. "I guess it's like everything else. There're advantages and disadvantages. What about your mother? You never mention her."

C. J. pushed her plate away. "She died when I was twelve."

Lois's hand reached toward her but stopped short. "I'm sorry. It must've been rough growing up without a mother. I can't imagine losing mine even now."

"Dad filled in wherever he could. He's really great."

"You look a lot like your father. You both have those big doe eyes." Lois was looking at her closely.

C. J. met her gaze and smiled. Lois turned her attention to pushing the last of her coleslaw around with her fork. "He means a lot to you, doesn't he?"

C. J. brushed the hair away from her face. She had been so busy she hadn't had time to get it trimmed. "He's always been there for me. After Mom died." She hesitated. She didn't like talking about her mother. There were still too many things she hadn't resolved. "He's always been there," she repeated lamely. "As a teenager I never had many friends. The girls were all boy crazy, and that held absolutely no interest for me. And the boys, well, like I said, they were of no interest to me." She gave a sharp laugh. "I never liked the kids who were my social peers. They were all so boring. I liked to run around with the kids from Fort Sam. They did really neat stuff. I remember having one close friend, Tina. Her mom was a maid for the people next door, and Tina used to sit on the back doorstep while her mom worked on Saturdays. We would sneak off and play in the woods behind our house until her mom caught us playing a very interesting version of house." C. J. smiled at the memory and drained her beer. "Tina never came back. I finally got brave enough one day to go over and ask her mom where she was. She told me she thought it was best if Tina didn't stray so far out of her class." C. J. shook her head in bitter memory.

"My poor little rich girl," Lois chuckled.

C. J. remembered how angry the comment had made her a few weeks ago. Tonight she simply shrugged and smiled.

Lois sat back abruptly and tossed her napkin on the table. "I've had a great time, but I have to get to bed. My shift starts at six tomorrow."

To hide her disappointment, C. J. signaled for their checks.

C. J. had parked near Lois's truck, and they walked out together.

"When will you be back from your trip?" Lois asked.

"A week from tomorrow," C. J. replied as they stopped beside Lois's truck. A warm breeze blew Lois's hair across her face. Her innocent gesture of brushing it away destroyed all of C. J.'s good intentions. She leaned into Lois and gently kissed her. "I'd like to see you when I get back." She was now certain beyond a doubt that Ron was wrong. She would give up everything for Lois.

Lois stepped away. "C. J., I told you before that I'm not interested in dating you."

"I'm trying to be more responsible," C. J. argued.

"It's for three months while your father rests. What happens after that?"

C. J. knew she couldn't give her an honest answer. "I don't know," she said and shrugged.

"I need stability and commitment," Lois reminded her.

"I think I can give you that," C. J. said, placing a hand on Lois's waist. She looked into her eyes. "Will you at least give me a chance?"

Lois tucked her hands into the pockets of her jeans and gazed at the sky before looking back at C. J. "I'm already seeing someone."

C. J. felt the breath leave her as she stepped away. When she could speak she asked, "Is it serious?"

"It's too soon to tell, but I hope it is."

"I see." C. J. stubbed the toe of her tennis shoe against the gravel. An awkward silence fell between them. Finally C. J. squared her shoulders. "I should be leaving. I still have to pack," she lied. "Maybe the three of us can get together for dinner some time."

Lois shrugged again, "Maybe."

"Good-bye." C. J. moved toward her car.

"Bye."

She waited for Lois's truck to leave before letting the tears fall.

C. J. slowly made her way home. Why had she been so stupid? She hadn't meant to kiss Lois. She slapped the steering wheel. Of all the women in the world, why did she have to fall in love with one who didn't want her?

The house was dark when she pulled into the driveway. The front porch bulb must have blown out, or maybe Alice had forgotten to turn it on. C. J. sighed when she remembered it was Alice's day off and her father wasn't there to turn the light on.

C. J. felt a tinge of uneasiness as she stepped from her car and started up to the house. None of the front lights were on. The floodlights in the front garden should have turned on automatically at sundown. She thought about going back to her car and calling the police, but the idea seemed too silly. She fumbled with the key and finally got the door open. When she flipped the switch to the inside light, the room was flooded with soft light. She realized she had been holding her breath, and she exhaled loudly. She was about to lock the door when car lights swung into the driveway. Still feeling a little tense, she started to close the door until she saw that it was James's Mercedes.

She waved as James stepped from the car and made his way up the steps.

"Hello," she called and wondered what he was doing out. She was much closer to Ron than to James.

"Hello, C. J.," he said and leaned down to kiss her cheek. She was shocked by the dark circles under his eyes.

"You look like you could use a drink," she said, closing the door behind him and automatically locking it.

"That would be great."

"Scotch, right?" C. J. asked as she led him into her father's study.

He dropped to the couch as though the weight of the world was pressing down on his shoulders.

C. J. stood before him, holding out the glass of Scotch for several seconds. "James." He didn't respond, and she leaned forward and touched his arm. "Are you okay?" she asked, suddenly scared. Had Ron left after all?

James looked up at her and took the drink. He took a small sip before downing the entire drink and handing the glass back to her.

C. J. refilled the glass and handed it to him. "What's up?" she asked, not really wanting to hear.

"I think Ron is going to leave me," he said in a voice hardly more than a whisper. He looked at the drink and set it aside.

C. J. remained silent. She didn't know what to say or do. She couldn't lie to him, and she certainly couldn't tell him the truth.

"I came home early twice this week, and he wasn't home either time. When I asked where he had been, he went berserk." James looked at her. "I wasn't asking to check on him." He shrugged. "I've encouraged

him to get out more and get involved in something."
He rubbed his hands over his face. "It looks like he
finally has."

His shoulders began to shake, and C. J. moved to
the couch beside him.

"James," she began. "Ron would never leave you."
For a moment C. J. wanted to throttle Ron for putting
all of them in this position. Did James know or
suspect that Ron stayed with him because of the
luxuries James's income could provide?

He took C. J.'s hand and patted it. "You're a good
friend," he said finally.

C. J. looked away and felt miserable.

James took a deep breath and wiped his eyes with
a handkerchief from his pocket. "C. J., I know there
are other men in his life," he stated. He removed his
hand from her arm and wiped his eyes once more
before returning the handkerchief to his pocket.

"You're talking crazy," C. J. insisted. "Ron would
be a fool to leave you. Who else would put up with
him sitting at home all day?" She realized how close
her words were to the truth and stopped suddenly.
"What I mean is . . ." Words failed her, and she
floundered to a halt.

"Don't feel bad," James said. "I've always
suspected that Ron is more interested in my money
than he is in me."

"James, that isn't true." C. J. felt compelled to
argue, but he waved aside her protests.

"I'm ten years older than Ron. I was long past
being ready to settle down when I met him, and he
was just starting to play." He picked up the glass of
Scotch and took a small drink. "I thought he would

eventually get it out of his system and be contented with me. But now I'm beginning to wonder. He seems to be serious about this guy."

"You mean the golf pro wasn't the first guy?" C. J. blurted. She cringed when she realized she had just admitted to knowing about Ron's most recent infidelity. "How could he be so stupid?" C. J. fumed. "With AIDS and everything that can happen now. Why do you stay with him?"

"I love him," James stated simply. "He promised me he was always careful, and we rarely . . ." He stopped, his face flushing slightly. "What I mean is . . ." He set the glass on the table.

"It's okay," C. J. assured him, not wanting to know any more about his and Ron's sex life. "Have you talked to him?" C. J. asked after an awkward silence.

James nodded. "He says there's no one else. That it's just my imagination." His eyes were beginning to tear. "C. J., I don't want to live without him."

She took his hand and looked directly into his eyes. "You won't have to," she promised. "No matter what, Ron won't leave you."

For a moment they stared at each other, and C. J. saw realization slowly hit James. A brief look of pain crossed his face before he gave a weak smile.

"Thank you," he said and squeezed her hand. He stood abruptly and ran a hand over his thick, dark hair.

James would be considered a handsome man from anyone's point of view. He was successful and he was kindhearted. Who could ask for more?

"James," she said as he turned to leave.

"Yeah."

"Money isn't everything. Maybe you should take more time to enjoy what you have."

He looked at her and frowned before finally giving a small nod and leaving.

C. J. followed him to the door and hugged him good-bye. After locking up and setting the alarm, she slowly climbed the stairs to her room.

She sat on the side of her bed and tugged her shoes off. She was thinking about Ron when she noticed a peculiar odor. She wrinkled her nose at the faint stench. She tried to place it, but thoughts of Lois began to push in to compete with her concern for James and Ron. Finally she gave up on trying to solve anything. She stripped out of her clothes and dropped them to the floor. She stood in the shower, slowly alternating between extremely hot and extremely cold water until she felt her tense muscles begin to relax.

When she stepped back into her bedroom, she gathered up her crumpled clothes and dropped them into the hamper before picking up her shoes and placing them in the closet. Without allowing any more thoughts of Ron, James, or Lois to intrude, she crawled into bed and fell into a restless sleep.

C. J. and Mary had rented a car and were driving around the valley to talk to growers about purchasing their crops. C. J. made certain she was too busy to think about Lois. She and Mary had no set agenda and often went to visit one grower on a suggestion from another one. That's how they ended up in Brownsville at ten-thirty at night with no hotel reservations.

Every hotel in town was full due to the National Dairyman's Convention. It was eleven-thirty before they found a motel on the highway that had a vacancy — a single.

"We could drive on to Harlingen," C. J. suggested, staring at the small bed. Up until now they had booked separate rooms each night. She still wasn't sure how Mary felt about her lesbianism.

"I'm so tired I can't go another mile," Mary swore. "If you have no major objections, I say we stay here."

C. J. sat on the lone bed while Mary finished in the bathroom. She now wished she had insisted they drive on.

In an attempt to make everything seem as normal as possible. C. J. placed her nightly call to Janice's voice mail at the office and left her instructions for several items that needed to be attended to. She also gave her the name and phone number of the motel they were staying in.

Mary emerged in a short gown, yawning. "All yours," she muttered, heading for the bed.

As C. J. was closing the door, Mary bent to turn the cover back, giving C. J. a view of long, smooth thighs. A view that sent C. J. directly into a cold shower.

C. J. crawled into bed wearing a pair of shorts and a long shirt. She was so cold from the shower that her teeth were chattering. Since she normally slept nude and had not anticipated these sleeping arrangements, she hadn't brought anything to sleep in. She clung to the edge of the bed and listened to Mary's even breathing. *At least she's asleep,* she sighed. Exhaustion soon overtook her, and she drifted off to sleep.

A warm hand was caressing her breasts. *A nice dream. That could be Lois's hand.* She snuggled closer to it. The hand continued to caress her, moving inside the band of her shorts. Lips brushed her ear. "C. J."

C. J.'s eyes flew open at Mary's voice. The hand was still moving inside her shorts, and a tongue was tracing her ear.

"Oh god," she cried, sitting up in bed.

"What's wrong?" Mary jerked back to avoid being hit by C. J.'s head.

"I'm sorry. I was asleep. I didn't mean..." C. J. was confused. Somehow in her sleep she had managed... to what? Get Mary's hand in her shorts and lips on her ears? C. J. snapped on the bedside lamp.

"What's wrong?" Mary asked again.

C. J.'s thoughts raced. Was Mary pretending it never happened? Or worse, had she been dreaming? C. J. rubbed her hands over her face, trying to sort out the events.

"It's all right." Mary reached for her and pulled her against her. "It's all right," she whispered again, kissing C. J.'s hair. A hand brushed down C. J.'s back, sending waves of desire through her.

C. J. pulled away. "Mary, I can't."

Mary laughed and kissed her softy. "I know you don't believe in commitments."

"But I do," C. J. stuttered. "Or at least I want to."

Mary frowned. "Is there someone special?"

C. J. thought of Lois, but Lois wasn't interested in her. She was interested in someone else. "No."

"Then what's the problem?" Mary pulled her short

gown over her head. C. J. stared at the luscious body as waves of desire shot through her. If Lois didn't want her and Mary did, then what was the problem? Mary's hand sliding up C. J.'s thigh made her decision. She pulled her shirt off and slid the shorts off her hips.

Mary stared in appreciation as she ran her fingertips slowly up the inside of C. J.'s legs. "You have no idea how often I've thought of doing this to you."

C. J. moaned and ran her hands down Mary's back. "You always seemed so," C. J. paused searching for the appropriate word, "straight."

Mary silenced her with a long, deep kiss. Her lips trailed across C. J.'s throat and back up to her ear. C. J. pulled her on top of her. She gasped as Mary slid slowly down her body until her mouth greedily claimed a breast. Her warm tongue sent waves of pleasure through C. J. as it encircled a hardened nipple. C. J.'s legs wrapped around Mary as her body arched up seeking release.

"Not yet," Mary whispered.

"Yes," C. J. groaned.

Mary extracted herself and continued to slide her tongue down C. J.'s burning body. She ran it across the top of thin, brown pubic hair and then nipped her way down C. J.'s thigh and back up her other thigh.

C. J. tried to grab her head, but Mary eluded her to again start her journey down between the long, slender legs.

The ache in C. J.'s body escalated as Mary's tongue traced the tender field behind her knee. "Now," she begged, reaching for her.

Again Mary ignored her as she kissed her way back up. Her breath scorched C. J.'s aching hunger.

Mary once more kissed and tongued a triangular outline around C. J.'s throbbing center as C. J. cried out her need.

"Now," Mary relented, grabbing C. J.'s hips and plunging her tongue deep into the creamy desire. C. J. groaned, digging her heels into the bed and pushing urgently against her. Long slender fingers slid slowly in and out.

"Harder," C. J. begged as the fingers once more moved in to claim her. Mary sucked C. J. deeper and deeper into her mouth while her plunging fingers became almost brutal in their attack.

The image of Lois's face floated before C. J., and her body exploded into a wave of pleasure. Before the first wave left, a second one began, causing her to push urgently against Mary's mouth and tongue. In an urgent need to be closer, she sat upright, and rolled Mary over and rode the final wave of pleasure. With her own screams of passion still ringing in her ears, C. J. fell over and pulled Mary's body up to her. Their exhaustion was forgotten as they made love until both fell into a sated slumber.

CHAPTER SIX

The phone jarred C. J. awake. Sunlight was filtering through a slight crack in the drapes. Her first thought was that she had been unfaithful to Lois. She shook her head in disgust. How could she have been unfaithful to Lois when Lois wanted nothing to do with her? She picked up the receiver on the third ring.

"Hello."

"C. J., this is Janice."

"Hi." She stifled a yawn. "I was going to call you after breakfast, to check in."

"Breakfast. It's ten-thirty already."

"Shit." C. J. grabbed her watch. "We overslept. We were up most of the night looking for a room. There's a National —"

Janice interrupted her. "C. J., I don't care. Listen, we have a problem. One of the warehouses on Houston Street burned last night, and they attempted to burn another one."

C. J. felt her palms begin to sweat. She didn't need problems to start happening now. "Was anyone hurt?"

"No. The night watchman was patrolling between the buildings. He saw the blaze and called the fire department. He managed to put one out himself, but the other one was too far gone by the time the fire department arrived. They're ruling it as arson."

C. J. snapped on the lamp and sat up. Mary stretched and began rubbing C. J.'s back.

"Arson. Someone deliberately set it?" C. J. asked.

Mary sat up in bed and was trying to hear the other end of the conversation by pressing her ear close to the phone. "Janice, hold on a minute." She quickly gave Mary the highlights.

Mary hopped from the bed and began gathering their clothes. "Tell her we're coming back today."

"Janice, we're coming back. Make our flight arrangements."

"I already have. Your flight leaves from Harlingen in an hour."

"That doesn't give us a lot of time," C. J. said, swinging her feet out of bed.

"It was either that or midnight," Janice informed her.

C. J. hung up the phone and sat collecting her

thoughts. Guilt over Lois would have to wait. Mary was tossing her clothing into a suitcase. C. J. pulled on a pair of jeans, trying to ignore the heat that was building between her legs as she watched Mary's nude body bend and sway. There was no time for a repeat of last night. Mary was another issue she would have to come to terms with soon. She wondered what it would be like waking up to the same person each morning. She tried to picture Mary as that person, but Lois's face kept intruding.

They arrived at the airport in plenty of time for the early flight back to San Antonio. Both fell asleep soon after takeoff. C. J. woke as they were preparing to land. Mary closed her notebook computer and smiled, watching as C. J. stretched her cramped muscles.

"How about dinner tonight?" C. J. asked as the plane taxied in.

Mary began collecting her papers. "I'm going to be too busy. Maybe another time."

C. J. placed her hand over Mary's. "I read somewhere that sex stimulates the brain cells."

Mary gazed at her. "I thought we both understood that last night was nothing more than a distraction."

C. J. felt her face turn scarlet. What was wrong with her? Now that she was ready to settle down and be a responsible adult, no one wanted her. In less than a month she had been told to take a hike by three women. Being left was a new experience for her. She normally did the leaving. She realized Mary was waiting for her to say something. *At least leave with grace,* she told herself. "Yeah, sure. I just thought you might like to discuss the new accounts we got this week."

Mary visibly relaxed. "There'll be plenty of time to take care of that tomorrow." She busied herself, putting her notebook away. "I want to get home to Tom."

"Tom!" Several nearby passengers turned to stare. C. J. lowered her voice and leaned closer to her. "You're married?"

"No," Mary said and shuffled her papers into a neat stack. "We're living together."

C. J. threw her arms up in exasperation and ignored the stares. "Oh, great. Now I feel much better. You're only bisexual."

Mary's mouth hardened as she fixed C. J. with a cold glare. "Do you have a problem with that? And lower your voice. People are staring."

C. J. lowered her voice. "Hell yes I have a problem with that. I don't remember any mention of Tom last night."

"Get over it," Mary hissed. She threw her notes into the briefcase and snapped it shut.

The plane had landed, and people were beginning to depart.

"Why didn't you tell me?" C. J. demanded.

"I didn't see where it was an issue."

C. J. forced herself to remain silent as they made a stormy exit to Mary's car in the long-term parking lot.

"What exactly is your problem?" Mary demanded after she paid the parking attendant and pulled out into traffic. "Are you pissed that there's someone else or because the someone else is a man?"

C. J. stared out the window. She wasn't sure which

issue upset her most. She had always made it a point not to date women who were already involved. Of course, she had no qualms about dating more than one woman at a time. She felt this was fair since she always made it clear up front that she was not looking for a relationship.

"C. J., look at me." Mary's hand touched C. J.'s arm briefly as C. J. turned from the window. "I thought you understood that I wasn't looking for a commitment," Mary said and glanced at her. "I find you very attractive, but I don't want the insecurities of a lesbian relationship."

C. J. bristled, and Mary held her hand up to stop her. "I only got involved with you because I was under the impression that you preferred one-night stands. Rumor has it that you never date any woman for more than a month."

"You shouldn't believe everything you hear," C. J. said, her voice thick with hurt. She suddenly recalled Lois's comment about her driving record being the talk of the San Antonio Police Department. "When did my life become a public record?"

Mary stared at her. "The day you were born." She shook her head and added with a thick touch of sarcasm, "I guess being the daughter of a millionaire does have a few drawbacks."

C. J. started to throw back a remark, but they were nearing the Riley home. She knew she had to repair the damage. She and Mary had to work together, and now was not the time to let sex muddy their working relationship. Mary was right in believing C. J. had never been willing to commit to anyone. So why was this bothering her so? Was it because Mary was controlling the situation, or had something in

C. J. changed? She shrugged off the thoughts. There wasn't time to sort this mess out now. She had to settle things between them, and it wasn't Mary's fault.

"I'm sorry," C. J. conceded. "I guess this mess with the warehouses has me a little on edge. You're right. I'm not looking for a relationship. Let's forget about it, okay?"

Mary reached across the seat and squeezed her hand. "Thanks. I really do like you, C. J." With a sultry look she added, "You're one of the hottest women I've ever known."

C. J. bit back a question of exactly how many that had been.

The police had been unable to find any new evidence regarding the warehouse fires. They assured C. J. that a homeless person seeking shelter probably started it and that the fire wasn't directed specifically at Riley Produce. C. J. wasn't comfortable with the reasoning. After all, it was much too warm for anyone to need a fire for warmth. She finally conceded that perhaps someone had been trying to cook over an open flame. Riley Produce wouldn't be out any great expense. The insurance would cover most of the damage to the warehouses and their contents.

C. J. thought about the phone calls that came in every afternoon just after Janice left. Could they somehow be connected? She was certain that if she mentioned the calls now the police would think she was being paranoid, so again she decided not to mention them.

Maybe she should call Lois and ask her opinion.

But what if the other woman answered? The questions that had been plaguing C. J. started again. Were Lois and this woman living together? If not, how often did they see each other? C. J. felt panic rising in her chest. She couldn't think about Lois. It was time to forget about her.

CHAPTER SEVEN

C. J. pulled her Jag out of the parking lot. It was after seven, and traffic was light. Not wanting to go home to an empty house, she drove with no destination in mind.

Her father would be back in three weeks, and it was time for her to make some decisions. She discovered she enjoyed working, but she wasn't sure where she would fit in at Riley Produce. She definitely didn't want to return to her previous token position.

She enjoyed the challenge of the responsibilities that Riley's demanded. And although she loved her father, she didn't think they could work that closely together. He would always attempt to protect and coddle her. Having gotten a small taste of freedom from that overprotection, she found she enjoyed it.

Discovering her own strengths and abilities had given C. J. a sense of confidence she had never known before. Real confidence, not just the cocky bluster she had gotten by on for so many years.

She didn't kid herself. She knew that without Janice's and Mary's help she would never have gotten through the previous two and a half months. But there was enough of C. J.'s own efforts there to make her feel good about what she had accomplished. The company was meeting orders on time and with quality produce. Her father was getting the rest he needed and deserved.

C. J. hadn't told him about Ray quitting or about the fires. There would be plenty of time when he returned. Mary was doing a much better job in Ray's position than he had, and Sylvia Longoria had been promoted into Mary's old position with barely a ripple in the changeover.

There was the matter of the warehouse burning down, but that would have happened even if her father had been there, so C. J. didn't consider it a failure on her part. She acted quickly in renting another warehouse, and they had only been late on three orders because of the produce lost in the fire.

As for her personal life, Mary had made no further mention of their sexual encounter, and C. J. found she was grateful. Mary was a beautiful woman, but they weren't meant to be. Her thoughts turned to Lois as they did so often.

After an hour of random driving, she found herself

near where Lois lived. She considered dropping by. Would Lois mind? C. J. eyed the phone lying on the seat next to her. Maybe it would be better to call first. She reached for the phone, thought of Lois's new lover, and lost her nerve. Instead she pulled into a convenience store for a soda. As she walked away from her car, she was vaguely aware of another car pulling along beside her.

Inside the convenience store she walked to the back where the sodas were kept in a large cooler that spanned the width of the building. Maybe she would give Lois a call and invite them both to dinner. A masochistic streak within her wanted to meet this woman that Lois seemed so keen on.

As C. J. walked up to the cash register, she vaguely noticed the male cashier and a woman who was clutching a small boy to her. They were staring at something C. J. could not see from her vantage point. Her thoughts were still locked on Lois. Her response to their strange behavior was slow. It wasn't until she was nearly on them that she saw Ray Mason and the pistol he was now pointing at her.

"Ray," she gasped. Her heart began to pound against her ribs.

"Glad you could join us, Ms. C. J. Riley." He smiled a sick smirk and motioned with the weapon for her to stand with the other two. "You didn't even notice me following you, did you, dyke?" He stepped toward her.

The woman stared at C. J. with a look of near horror and moved away from her, clutching her son. C. J. shook her head in amazement. Here was a fool with a gun, and the woman was worried about standing next to a dyke!

C. J. turned her attention back to the pistol and tried to control the shaking in her voice. "What's going on here, Ray? Put the gun down before someone gets hurt." She noticed his appearance for the first time. He was no longer the Ray Mason she had known. He had several days' growth of beard, and she could smell the sour stench of his unwashed body. A cold glint was in his hate-filled eyes.

"You took everything away from me. My job, my wife, everything," he rasped.

"I had nothing to do with your wife leaving you. She left you a year ago, remember?" C. J. reasoned. *Where in the hell were the police when you needed them?* Her hands were trembling so she could barely hold the soda can.

"It was a pervert like you that corrupted her and made her leave."

The woman placed her hands over her son's ears.

"Your wife left you for a woman?" C. J. blurted, momentarily forgetting her terror. She didn't have time to fully comprehend the news before he sprang forward and stuck the pistol beneath her chin. She was trapped against the counter and could feel the hands of the cashier steadying her. She and Ray stared at each other. A cold sweat ran down C. J.'s side. She knew he wanted to kill her. She could see it in his eyes. A million thoughts flew through her mind. The things she would never be able to do. Would Ray hurt the others? Surely even Ray wasn't crazy enough to hurt a child over his wife's infidelities. She thought about how she had let her father down again. If she died he would always blame himself. Her dad had trusted her to handle things, and she had failed him by botching the company's relationship with Ray. For a fleeting moment she wondered how Lois would feel about her death.

Ray pressed the pistol harder against C. J.'s chin. As his eyes bore into hers, something shifted inside C. J. Her knees shook less. Her breathing slowed, and an anger like nothing she had ever known before began to build. Something in her eyes or face must have changed because Ray frowned slightly and the pressure from the pistol lessened.

A noise drew their attention to the parking lot. A car had pulled up. Dazed, they all turned to watch as the unsuspecting man approached the store. He was alongside the Jag when Ray stepped back and fired through the glass. The man hit the ground and scrambled behind the car. Ray started toward the door but stopped as C. J. stepped forward.

He whirled to face her, his eyes wide. "I'm going to make you pay," he growled, waving the pistol. Flecks of spit were caught in his beard.

C. J. realized with a start that Ray Mason was insane. She was still holding the can of soda. Could she possibly throw it at him and get the gun? The sick smile slid across his face again, almost as if he had read her mind.

"Time to settle an old score," he said and pointed the pistol at her head.

"What then?" she asked. The sense of calmness still coursed through her. He stopped, looking confused. "What will you do then?" she asked again.

She had to find some way to distract him until help arrived. The man he had shot at would call the police, and they would be here soon. Then it occurred to her. She could give Ray a means to obtain what he had always wanted. Power. All she had to do was give

113

him the one thing that had always been prominent in her life. Money. He would need money. That was the one thing she had plenty of. She slowly set the soda on the counter.

"Ray, where will you go? That man" — she pointed toward the door — "will call the police. You'll never make it out of here if you hurt any of us. You'll need money, Ray. I can help." She gave him a minute to think.

The little boy was starting to whimper, and Ray glared at him. C. J. wanted to tell the woman to keep him quiet, but she was afraid to draw more attention to the child. She had to convince Ray to let the others go. Alone, maybe she could do something. She started to coax him again.

"My dad will give you whatever you ask for. Let these people go, and we'll call him."

"No. It's a trick." Ray began to pace back and forth in front of C. J. "Mr. Riley's gone."

"Ray, I won't trick you. We won't even have to wait for Dad. I'll call the bank myself. I'll do whatever it takes to get the money here. Just let everyone else go." C. J. could hear the desperation in her voice and took a deep breath to steady it.

A convoy of police cars began descending on the parking lot. Their lights flashed wildly through the store windows.

Ray groaned and waved madly for everyone to move to the back of the store. The little boy's whimpering became a full-blown cry, and he buried himself between his mother's legs. Ray was yelling for them to move. He grabbed the woman and pulled her against him. Turning, he stumbled into a display of batteries that fell over and slid across the floor. With the gun at the woman's head, he began dragging her to the back of the store. The screaming child was clinging to her dress and being pulled along with them.

"Keep away," Ray kept yelling toward the front of the store, his eyes wild.

The scene inside the store became total chaos. The woman was screaming, and the little boy was kicking at Ray and crying. Ray whirled about, wildly screaming threats. The cashier stepped behind C. J. She turned to him. He was no more than eighteen or nineteen. A parade of freckles marched across his pale face. C. J. nodded toward the door. He glanced back once. C. J. could see the conflict in his eyes. She gave him her sternest glare and again nodded at the door. He gave her one last look and fled.

C. J. stepped between Ray and the door. The cashier was already gone before Ray noticed. He shot toward the door again, and C. J. hit the floor.

The deafening noise of the shot silenced everyone. Ray stood staring at the pistol as though he had just discovered it. His arm was still wrapped around the woman's neck.

C. J. stood slowly and turned to Ray. "Listen to me, Ray. You have to let the woman and the boy go. They'll only get in your way, and if you hurt them the police won't let you leave. Let them go, and I'll get any amount of money you want."

Ray stood silent for some time, then motioned to a roll of duct tape that was on the shelf. "Get the tape," he growled.

C. J. did as she was told.

"Now tape her hands together. Behind her." He shoved the woman forward. The boy refused to let go of his mother and began to kick at C. J. as she tried to wrap the tape around the woman's wrists. "What's your name?" C. J. asked, wrapping the tape around the woman's wrists.

"Helen," she sobbed softly.

"And your son's?"

"Shawn."

"Helen, you have to settle Shawn down. It's only making Ray worse." She nodded toward Ray, who was staring intently at the gathering police cars outside.

"Shut up!" Ray shouted over his shoulder.

C. J. tossed the roll of tape aside and stood waiting.

"Sit her down over there." Ray turned and pointed to a spot on the floor.

C. J. slid Helen to the floor against the cooler and settled a still whimpering Shawn beside her. Helen began to talk softly to her son.

"You in the store." The amplified voice of the police made everyone jump. "Come out with your hands up."

C. J. wondered irritably if anyone had ever actually obeyed that asinine command.

"You'd better get back," Ray screamed. "I'll kill them all!" He fired two wild shots toward the front of the store. C. J. threw herself over Helen and Shawn, expecting a barrage of gunfire to be returned from the police. When nothing happened, she stood, embarrassed by her overreaction. Shawn stared at her.

"Guess I watch too much television," she offered and smiled at the bewildered boy. Ray was watching the front, and C. J. wondered if she could jump him. She was physically fit, but he did have a gun. She thought about the number of shots he had fired. Could he be running low on ammunition? How many bullets did a pistol hold anyway? He turned back toward her, and she found herself studying the weapon. She had no idea what it was, but there was no cylinder, and that meant it must have a clip. If so, it didn't take a gun expert to know he probably wasn't low on ammo.

Since television police procedures were the only point of reference she had to use, C. J. decided to give it a try.

"Ray, you have to make a decision soon. The police will fill this place with tear gas. If you let the woman and boy go, it'll show them you're willing to negotiate."

For a moment he looked like the Ray Mason she had known across a boardroom table, except for the vagueness in his eyes. "Negotiate," he said, his eyes glazing. "Yes. Negotiations are important. You can't sign a deal without negotiations."

C. J. took a step toward him and said, "Let me handle them for you. I'll convince them to bring you the money and let you leave. You can go anywhere you want. I'll let you have my Jag. There's not a car in Texas that can match its speed," she bragged and hoped she was wrong.

"They won't listen to you." His voice took on an almost whining tone.

She had to convince him that she could make the authorities give him anything he wanted. C. J. drew herself up and forced more bravado than she felt. "My father is Carlton Riley. They'll damn well do anything I say."

Helen's quiet murmurs to Shawn were the only sound within the store. C. J. could see Ray was thinking about it.

"You could be in Mexico in a matter of hours, with more money than you could ever spend," C. J. said and continued to edge toward him until he waved the pistol for her to stop.

"Just think of how jealous your ex-wife will be. She'll be sorry she left you then." C. J. prayed that he still wanted his ex-wife back. "She'll be begging you to take her back." She stopped in a panic. *I've gone too far*, she thought. *Not even Ray is stupid enough to believe that lie.*

To her relief, his eyes lit up, and C. J. cautiously continued. "Let me go talk to them."

"No!" Helen shouted, as she struggled to stand up. "You can't leave us alone with him! It's you he wants, not us! She won't come back," she yelled at Ray.

C. J. gave herself a mental kick for not taping Helen's mouth shut.

Ray's lip turned up in an ugly sneer. "Still only worrying about your own skin, aren't you, C. J.?"

C. J. shook her head and tried to speak, but he cut her off.

"Thought you had me convinced that Sue would come back to me, didn't you, dyke? Well, I don't want her back. She's dirty." His voice had taken on a low, almost conversational tone that C. J. found more frightening than his screaming.

C. J. refused to give up. She looked at Helen, but spoke to Ray. "I give you my word I'll return." Turning back to Ray she added, "Let me go out and talk to them. I'll get you the money, and you can leave."

He looked from C. J. to Helen. The flashing lights from the police cars were spinning madly around the room. He grinned and stepped closer to C. J. "I've had fun watching you. You didn't even know I had been in your house. I was on your bed. I touched your things. You know I can always find you again if you don't come back." He stepped still closer.

C. J. could smell the sour stench of his body. Her throat closed in fear and revulsion. She had smelled that peculiar odor before — in her room the night James had come by to talk to her. He was waiting for her to answer. All she could manage was to nod her acknowledgment.

"I was going to grab you that night, but the fag came by and I decided to wait. I've liked watching you," he leered. He leaned closer to her. His breath was hot against her cheek. She forced herself to stand still and not back away from him.

"Do you realize I can get you any time I want to?"

"Yes."

He looked toward the front of the store. "They won't catch me because I'm smarter than they are," he assured her. He turned back to her and grinned. "You will be back, won't you?"

"Yes," C. J. answered, too afraid to say anything more.

"This is just so they'll know I'm serious and to remind you who's in control here." He slammed the butt of the pistol into C. J.'s forehead. Pain blinded her as she fell to the floor. She was vaguely aware of Helen screaming, and of Shawn's thin, high-pitched screams mixing with his mother's.

Ray's laughter echoed in her ears as she fought the darkness that was engulfing her. She pressed her aching forehead against the cool floor that smelled of years of wax and ancient cigarette smoke. Ray grabbed her arm and yanked her to her feet.

His mouth was against her ear. "Now, you go tell them to have a million in small, used bills here by midnight. They're to bring it to the door in a suitcase. Every car is to be out of the parking lot, except for the Jag. And I want the road cleared of all traffic from here to Interstate 37." He pushed the pistol under her chin. "Be sure to remind them that I have the woman and kid. And you know what I'll do to them if you don't come back, don't you?"

Helen was sobbing. Blood was running down C. J.'s face. He shook her until she nodded her head and said, "I'll tell them." Her voice sounded thick and distant. Ray shoved her down the aisle toward the door.

Helen sobbed harder. "Don't leave us," she begged.

C. J. looked back into Helen's haunted eyes. "I'm coming back," she promised. She held on to the shelves for balance. Using her free hand she tried to wipe the blood from her forehead, but it kept streaming. As she neared the door she could see people running around in the parking lot. She decided she'd better let them know she was one of the good guys. She slowly raised her hands. She pushed through the door and was met by a warm gentle breeze. A sudden exhilarating feeling of freedom brought tears to her eyes.

CHAPTER EIGHT

"C. J., move this way," a familiar voice called from the darkness to her left. It was Lois. C. J.'s heart pounded, and she had to fight the urge to run to her. She moved toward the voice, blood trickling into her eye. She wiped at it and stumbled.

There was a movement to her right, and Lois was there pulling C. J. into the safety of darkness against the side of the building. Lois's arms were around her, providing a circle of security. "What's wrong with your head? Why are you bleeding? How bad are you hurt? It's too dark to see."

"He hit me. I'll be all right." C. J. began to tremble.

"Are you sure?"

"I'm scared," she answered, trying to make it sound like a joke, but it came out a choked sob.

"You're all right now." Lois's lips brushed against her ear. "I got here as fast as I could. The cashier recognized your name, and it went out over the radio that you were one of the hostages. I was so scared." She hesitated as C. J. was struck by a wave of uncontrollable shaking.

"I'm sorry," Lois apologized, her voice trembling. "I know this isn't the time. I've been so scared." She hugged C. J. again. "Come on. Let's get you to a medic."

"No. I have to . . ."

Lois wasn't listening. She was rushing C. J. away. They approached an ambulance and were quickly surrounded by people in a multitude of uniforms. A paramedic began working on her forehead as a volley of questions were fired at her. C. J. held up her hand to ward them off.

"Leave her alone for a minute," Lois snapped. Everyone fell silent, and C. J. began to relax. "C. J.," Lois started, "we need to know as much as possible about what's going on inside. Tell us what you can."

C. J. gave her a brief overview of what had occurred in the store. The cashier had already told them everything that had happened before he fled, so she focused on the later events. Then she told them of Ray's demands.

"A million dollars," a man in a police uniform barked. "It's not going to happen. My men can fill the store with tear gas and we'll flush the son-of-a-bitch out."

"The woman and little boy are still in there," C. J. reminded them. "Ray is desperate enough to kill them. Someone get me a phone. It's going to take time to get the money together, and he wants it by midnight."

"We're not paying a ransom," the police officer informed her.

Anger sliced through her. "Who are you?" she yelled as she shoved the paramedic away and jumped up. She could feel the heat of Lois's hand on her back.

"I'm Captain Avery, SAPD, and until the SWAT unit arrives, I'm in charge of this operation."

"No, Captain, you are *not* in charge," C. J. blazed. "The lunatic holding the gun inside that store is in charge and will be until that woman and child are free. Now find me a damn phone."

"I won't allow you to pay the ransom," Captain Avery declared. "Besides, no one can get that much money together on such short notice."

"I can and I will," C. J. insisted, holding his gaze. There was no time to waste arguing with this fool. "Unless you would prefer to explain your decisions to the press. I'm sure they're waiting for a story." She nodded to a group of news cameras that were being kept several yards away. "Maybe I should go talk to them."

He glared at the press before turning back to her. C. J. pushed hard. "It'll certainly make an interesting story if he kills them and I tell the press you refused to let me give him my money." She gave him a way out if he wasn't too bullheaded to use it.

123

"Do you intend to put up the money?" he snapped.

"Yes."

"Get her to a phone," he growled.

C. J. looked at her watch; it was eight-thirty-seven. There wasn't much time.

Twenty minutes and several arguments later she had made arrangements with the president of her father's bank for the money to be delivered. He kept telling her it was impossible, and she had finally told him to get the money or be prepared to lose Riley Produce as a customer. She knew he'd get the money together somehow. She was waiting for confirmation from the authorities that the road would be cleared, then all she had to do was tell them she was going back inside.

She looked up at the clouds rolling thickly across the sky. It would rain before morning, and hopefully before it came this nightmare would be over. All she had to do was go back inside and assure Ray that he would get everything he wanted. He would release them then. He had nothing to gain by keeping them.

C. J. was acutely aware of Lois hovering near her. They had been surrounded by people and hadn't been able to talk. C. J. deliberately kept her attention focused elsewhere. She couldn't afford to let herself think of Lois now. Lois wasn't going to be happy to learn that C. J. was going back into the store.

Captain Avery returned from a conversation with several state and city police officers. He grudgingly assured her that all of Ray's demands would be met at least until the hostages were free. C. J. slid off of the hood of the police car she had been sitting on. "I'm going back in," she announced.

"No!" Lois grabbed her arm.

"Absolutely not. The fewer hostages he has, the better off we are. We'll let him know over the speaker that his demands are being met," Avery stated.

"I'm going back," C. J. insisted. "It was part of the deal. He'll let the woman and child go if I go back in."

"If you even try to go back in there, I'll have you taken into protective custody." Captain Avery said and hooked his thumbs over his belt.

C. J. stared at him. He was gloating. "He won't believe you," she argued. "I'm trying to tell you, he said he'd let the woman and boy go if I came back."

"He's lying," Lois said and squeezed C. J.'s arm tighter.

C. J. forced herself to meet Lois's gaze. The light from the back of the ambulance showed the fear in Lois's eyes. "I'm sorry," C. J. whispered, "but I have to go back."

C. J.'s brain was screaming at her. *She doesn't want you to go back in there. So stay here!* C. J. stepped past Lois. *I can't believe I'm actually doing this*, C. J. marveled. What kind of fool would go back in there?

"Officer Franklin, place Ms. Riley in protective custody until someone can take her home," Avery said. His lips formed a smug smile.

Lois's hand rested on C. J.'s arm. C. J. pulled away and started for the store, but Lois grabbed her arm again. C. J. tried to break free, but Lois hands clamped on both arms and pulled her away from the crowd and back into the darkness by the side of the building.

C. J. continued to struggle until Lois spoke.

"Stop struggling and I'll let you go. I want to talk to you."

C. J. stopped fighting, and Lois slowly released her grip. They stood in silence. The darkness was so dense C. J. could only see vague outlines of things around them. She became painfully aware of how close Lois was standing to her. She could feel Lois's breath on her neck. She turned slowly and took a step back. Lois took C. J.'s arms again, but this time she held rather than restrained.

C. J. prayed that her voice would not betray her fear of returning to the store. "I have to go," she whispered.

Lois was facing her, still holding her by both arms. C. J. heard her take a deep breath and slowly exhale.

"C. J., I know this isn't the time, but I have to tell you now that I lied. There's no one else. I was attracted to you the first time I saw you. I couldn't stop thinking about you, but I was afraid of getting involved with you." Lois's arms continued clutching her. Stunned, C. J. let them support her as Lois continued. "I thought that if I told you there was someone else you'd go away and leave me alone. Then when you did I almost went crazy." Lois hesitated, and C. J. thought she heard a break in Lois's voice. She desperately wished she could see Lois's face. "I won't let you go back in there," Lois stated.

Could Lois really be saying what C. J. was hearing? C. J. pushed away the thoughts. She couldn't let herself think about anything but Helen and Shawn right now. She knew Ray would kill them if she didn't return. *He might anyway*, an inner voice nagged.

"You can't stop me." C. J. spoke around the knot in her throat.

"You're in police custody," Lois reminded her.

"Lois. Just look the other way for a minute."

In the darkness, Lois's lips met hers. Her arms slid around C. J. and pulled her closer. Every fiber of C. J.'s being screamed for her to stay here in the safety of Lois's arms. For a moment she gave in and melted into her, until she remembered the haunted looked in Helen's eyes. She pulled away.

"Please," Lois begged. "Don't even think of going back in there. He's already hurt you. He could ..." her voice trailed off.

"I promised," C. J. mumbled, still reeling from the kiss.

"Promised!" Lois exploded. "Nobody will blame you for not following through on that promise."

Lois's arms were too comfortable. One more kiss like that last one and C. J. felt sure she would lose all of her courage and not be able to go back in. She had to put space between herself and Lois. She tried to move away, but Lois's grip tightened.

Okay, C. J. told herself, *if I can't get physical distance, then I'll have to at least put some emotional distance between us.* She forced herself to think of every nasty comment Lois had ever made to her. It wasn't working, so C. J. forced her attention back to their conversation.

"I thought you wanted me to be more responsible and to realize that the world doesn't revolve around me. What was it you said? A promise is a promise?" She tried to pull away.

"Don't pull away from me," Lois said and ran her

hand along C. J.'s arm. "I only wanted you to face reality, not get yourself killed."

Suddenly exhausted, C. J. gave in and leaned her cheek against Lois's shoulder. "Lois, please try to understand. Right now, reality happens to involve a man with a gun. I have to go." She tried to pull away again, but Lois held firm.

"It's against every rule of law enforcement to allow you to go back in there. So give me one good reason why I should," Lois demanded.

For once, C. J.'s bluster failed her. She couldn't think of one smart comeback. So she answered as honestly as she could.

"Because I'll never be able to live with myself if I don't. Think about how you'd feel if our roles were reversed." The grip on C. J.'s arm eased, and C. J. started to walk away.

Lois's hand closed around her arm again. "You're determined to get me fired, aren't you?" Her hand moved to C. J.'s face. Her thumb brushed softly along C. J.'s cheek. "You'd damn well better come back," Lois said, her voice cracking.

C. J. pulled her close, and their lips met urgently in the darkness. "Will you be waiting for me when I come out?" C. J. asked, pulling away.

"Wild horses couldn't drag me away."

"Then I'll be back." C. J. promised and fled before her courage failed or common sense kicked in. She stood in the darkness at the corner of the building. There was no one other than Lois close enough to stop her. She took a deep breath and sprinted toward the store. She heard voices shouting for her to stop, but she was inside the store before they could get to her. The walk down the aisle seemed much longer than it had before, and the air conditioning felt cold and forbidding after the warm night air. The relief that showed in Helen's eyes made C. J. ashamed that she had even considered not returning.

Ray was sneering at her when she reached the end of the row he was hiding behind. "Well, C. J., it looks like I've misjudged you. Or maybe you just missed me too much, huh?" His laughter caused chills to course down her spine.

"Let them go," she said, trying to keep her voice steady.

"All in due time. Tell me what happened out there."

She pushed away the thoughts of Lois. "The money will be here by midnight. It'll be circulated bills of small denominations in a suitcase as you requested. All the cars except mine will be removed from the parking lot, and the roadway will be cleared to Interstate 37." She forced herself to meet his eyes. "You win, Ray. You're getting everything you asked for."

"This time I will." He grinned and ran the pistol barrel slowly down her cheek. She closed her eyes and clenched her teeth to keep from screaming. "Get me something to eat," he said, sliding his back along the end of the shelf until he sat on the floor. "Find me some chocolate chip cookies," he ordered.

C. J. searched the rows until she located the cookies. The door was only a few feet away. A quick dash and she could be out and with Lois again. She picked up the bag and walked back toward him. He laughed as she extended the bag to him. With deliberation she opened the bag and removed a handful of cookies before tossing the rest at him. She sat down beside Helen and handed Shawn the cookies. He looked at his mother, and she nodded. He grabbed the cookies and began to munch on them. Helen shifted and grimaced.

"Are you all right?" C. J. asked.

"My arms are going numb."

"Ray, let me undo her hands now."

"No."

"Why not?"

He flung a cookie at her. "Because I said no!"

"I'm okay," Helen said. They sat in silence for a few minutes. "Thank you for coming back," Helen said, focusing her gaze on Shawn. "I didn't think you would."

"I had a couple of doubts myself," C. J. admitted and smiled at Helen's surprised look.

For the next two and half hours they sat in silence. Shawn had crawled into his mother's lap and fallen asleep. C. J. envied him his innocence. She wondered how much of it had been shattered by this madman with a gun. She dropped her head onto her bent knees, careful to avoid the tender knot that had developed beneath the bandage.

She recalled the softness of Lois's lips and closed her eyes to allow the sensations of Lois's image to fully engulf her. She'd soon be free to leave. Her heart thudded wildly at the thought that within a matter of hours she could be tucked safely in bed with Lois. Her imagination was just beginning to explore those wonderful possibilities when Lois's voice cut through the night.

"Ray Mason. The item you requested has arrived."

Ray jumped to his feet, grabbed C. J., and pulled her up. He glanced at the clock on the wall and grinned. "Very good, *Ms. Riley*, it's only eleven forty-two. You've become very efficient."

"Let us go, Ray. You have what you want," C. J. pleaded.

"What's the matter? You tired of my company already?" His face was only inches from hers. She forced herself to not back away from his foul breath. "I know I can trust you," he whispered in her ear before shoving her toward the door. "Go get the suitcase and bring it here."

C. J. made the long journey down the aisle and once more stepped into the warm air.

Lois came forward and handed her the suitcase. "I'm supposed to keep you from going back in," she said, looking into C. J.'s eyes. "It seems everyone's a little more concerned about the daughter of Carlton Riley being a hostage than they are about the woman and kid. They think I can convince you not to return."

"Please don't ask," C. J. whispered, avoiding Lois's gaze. They were silent for several seconds.

"Did he say when he's going to release you?" Lois asked.

"As soon as the parking lot is clear of cars, I guess."

Lois's eyes held hers with a deep intensity. "The lot will soon be cleared of *cars*."

She had stressed the word *cars* a little too hard. Fear swept over C. J. as she realized what she meant. The cars would be gone, but the police wouldn't.

"If he sees anything he'll kill us," C. J. said in a panic. She had no doubt that Ray would do as he said.

"The SWAT team is in place. They won't do anything to jeopardize lives. They won't move unless they have a clear shot. Avery's no longer in charge," Lois assured her.

Lois looked toward the store. "C. J., have you ever fired a pistol?"

"No. Why?"

Lois shook her head and sighed. "Never mind. It was just a thought."

C. J. glanced down and noticed for the first time the small pistol tucked into Lois's belt. Her knees grew weak just thinking about what Lois was proposing. "I have to go," C. J. said quickly.

"I love you," Lois blurted.

C. J. stood rooted. Why did Lois have to tell her that now? C. J. wanted to grab Lois and run. Instead she forced herself to smile and wink. "I hope you've been thinking about our honeymoon." She saw the tears in Lois's eyes as she turned and walked back into the store.

Ray was still hiding at the end of the row. He grabbed her as she came within reach. "What took you so long? What was she saying?" he demanded, shaking her. He eyed the area where her shirt was tucked into her slacks. He grabbed her and swung her around, his hand roughly running along the band of her pants. She refused to think about what he might have done had he found a weapon.

She stood still until he was satisfied she wasn't hiding anything.

"What did she say?" he demanded again.

"She was telling me that the police are getting ready to leave and that the road has been cleared like you asked."

"Open the suitcase." He stood back as she lowered the case to the floor and opened it. C. J. heard Helen's sharp intake of breath as the lid was lifted to reveal the case full of money.

"Shall I count it?" she snapped.

Ray knelt and moved the stacks of bills around. "No, I think there should be enough to last me. If not, I can always come back for more, can't I?" She turned away from the bright gleam in his eyes.

C. J. noticed that the police cars were beginning to leave. "Let us go now while the police are still here. They'll see that you intend to keep your word."

He shook his head and continued to play with the money.

"Then at least let them go," she said, nodding to the woman and boy. "You still have me," she said. "I got you the money like I said I would, and the police are leaving. You're getting everything you wanted. Send them out."

He looked from Helen to the still sleeping Shawn and then to the door. Suddenly he waved the pistol toward the door. "Okay. Get out." He turned to C. J. "But you stay."

Helen tried to stand. C. J. ran to help her. C. J. shook Shawn awake. For once he remained silent as she helped Helen to her feet. As C. J. ripped the tape from her hands, Helen whispered, "I'll never forget what you've done for us tonight." With strips of the loose tape still dangling from her wrists, she gathered Shawn into her arms.

"Get going," C. J. said and shoved her forward. As mother and son raced out of the building, C. J. saw an arm reach out from the darkness and pull them from view. C. J. felt a sick feeling beginning to overtake her, but she pushed it away.

She turned to Ray, who was still kneeling on the floor looking at the suitcase of money.

"When are you going to let me go?" she demanded, kneeling down beside him. Through the doorway she could see the last of the police cars leave the parking lot.

"When?" she persisted. "We had a deal that I'd get you the money and you'd let us go."

"What's your hurry?" he asked, turning back to her. "It's just you and me now." Ray leered. "Or maybe that's what you've planned all along." He ran a hand along her leg. She rose and moved away. He closed the suitcase and stood holding it in his left hand. Ray grabbed her and pushed her toward a door marked employees only. C. J. fought against the fear that was rising inside her.

Once through the door he stood looking around before he shoved her into a corner and pulled a switch that sent the room into total darkness. Without warning, he was beside her.

"Now, isn't that better?" he whispered from behind her into her ear. The arm with the suitcase slid around her neck. C. J. tried to pull away, but he tightened his grasp and laughed. "Don't worry. There's no time for fun yet. We have to be going." He pushed her back out the door, suitcase banging awkwardly against her. When they reached the front of the store, C. J. realized the switch he had thrown must have controlled the outside lights as well. The parking lot was now in total darkness.

Ray tightened the grip around her neck. "Get your keys ready. You're driving."

Stunned, C. J. cried, "You said you'd let me go!" She cringed at the childish sound of her voice. Why hadn't she realized this sooner? Of course he couldn't let her go. He had to keep a hostage, and she had practically volunteered.

Ray's breath on her ear stopped her mental reprimand. "I changed my mind. I've decided to keep you around for a while. You see, I know why you came back." His tongue grazed her ear. She tried to pull away from him, but he laughed and held her tighter. As she fought against him she realized with sudden clarity that he intended to kill her. She wondered why he had allowed her to leave the store. Had he been that certain that she would return, or was he so insane that he was beyond any type of reasoning?

I'm not going to let him do it, she promised herself, and a sense of calmness settled over her. He eased the pressure around her neck and ran the hand with the gun across her breast. "Isn't this much better?" She forced herself not to pull away. "You'll just have to wait for the best part," he said, rubbing his crotch against her. C. J. swallowed the bile that rose in her throat.

Tightening his grip around her neck, he pushed her out the door. The thick cloud cover made the night unusually dark. C. J. could barely distinguish the outline of the Jag. As they neared the car, she pressed the button to deactivate the alarm. The normal tiny click rang out into the dark night, and the sudden flashing of the headlights sent Ray into a panic. He jumped and swung her in a wild circle.

"It was the alarm," she choked out. His arm was blocking her airway. "I can't breathe."

He relaxed his grip somewhat and pushed her toward the car. "Open the door," he whispered. She could smell his sweat and fear.

She opened the door, and the interior light flooded the area. He hid behind her, his back against the dimly lit car. His breath was blowing in ragged sheets against her neck. She cringed, waiting for the volley of gunfire to erupt, but nothing happened. Ray scrambled into the car backward, pulling her with him. As soon as he was inside he started screaming at her to shut the door. Somehow she managed to get inside and get the door closed with him still clinging to her, the suitcase, and the gun. As soon as the door closed they were again plunged into total darkness. He slid down below window level before releasing her and giving a series of nervous bursts of laughter. C. J. was sitting sideways in the seat with her feet drawn up under her chin. She started to struggle around in the cramped space. Ray grabbed her arm, but she jerked it away.

"If you want me to drive, I need to be facing forward!" She was angry with herself for being such a fool. *And a tall fool at that*, she spat. If she'd been shorter he couldn't have hidden behind her. She cursed the entire San Antonio police force for not performing one of those miracle rescues they were always showing on television.

"Let's go, but keep the lights off until I tell you to turn them on," he warned.

C. J. fastened her seat belt and for a wild instant prayed the car wouldn't start, but even the car let her down when the motor kicked over. She backed the car up and headed out of the parking lot. As Lois had promised, there wasn't a car in sight. C. J. strained her eyes, looking for hidden police officers, but saw only the darkness. They pulled onto the highway.

"I need the lights," C. J. said. "I can't see anything."

"Not yet."

A tire clicked over one of the reflectors that divided the lanes, and she kept driving on them until they reached an area with streetlights. The police had obviously cleared out everyone along the way. All of the businesses were closed with no one in sight. She realized that at this time of morning few of the businesses would have been open anyway. Five minutes later they were approaching Interstate 37.

"Head south," he said, sitting up and slipping on his seat beat before clutching the sides of the suitcase in his lap.

She tried not to think about what would happen to Riley Produce if he got away with the million dollars. "Can I turn the lights on?" she asked.

"Yeah."

C. J. turned on her lights and pulled onto the entrance ramp.

He shot forward. "There are cars!" he screamed, pointing the pistol at her.

Her heart pounded wildly. "You asked for the road to the interstate to be cleared, not the interstate itself," she reminded him. She glanced at him. Sweat soaked his shirt. She had to calm him down. "This is better," she reasoned. If we were the only car on the road, they'd know where we were. This way we can get lost in the rest of the traffic."

He seemed to think about it for a minute before being satisfied with her reasoning, and he settled back into an uneasy surveillance of every car around them. C. J. scanned the line of headlights in her rearview mirror. Which one of them would rescue her? They drove in silence for several minutes. Most of the would-be rescue cars passed or turned off without giving her a second look.

As they reached the Highway 181 cutoff, Ray motioned with his free hand. "Take this exit." He studied the cars behind them. C. J. watched the cars as well. No one followed them off.

"Where are we headed?"

"We'll head south long enough for them to think we're headed to Mexico." She was surprised that he answered. "Then we'll dump the car and I'll steal another one and head east. There're plenty of places for me to get lost on the East Coast."

C. J. didn't miss the fact that his pronouns were plural before they dumped the car and singular afterward. Apparently he intended to dispose of her and the car at the same time. They drove on in silence. With each passing mile, C. J. gave up the idea of a miracle rescue. She was on her own. She thought about her life, about her father, and about Lois. She hadn't had a bad life. There were certain areas she would change given the opportunity. Far ahead she saw a road sign announcing the approach of Loop 1604. How much farther would he want to drive? Maybe it was time to call his bluff.

"You intend to kill me, don't you?" she asked.

He turned, seemingly surprised at the question. "I was going to destroy Riley Produce at first. That's why I burned the warehouses. I was going to burn everything. Then I remembered that Mr. Riley couldn't help that you're a dyke any more than I could help that Sue . . ." He trailed off. He turned to stare at her through narrowed eyes. "You're sick and don't deserve to live." His reply was stated with such cold contempt that she shivered.

She forced her voice to sound calm and cold. "Loop 1604 is coming up."

"We're staying on this road," he muttered, staring out the window.

"It's called the death loop, you know." Once again she checked her rearview mirror. The only visible traffic was a pinpoint of lights in the far distance behind them. No one was going to help her. It was time for her to make a move. It was now or never. "Let's make it earn its name one more time," she said and pressed the accelerator to the floor. The car shot forward.

"What are you doing?" Ray demanded and pointed the pistol at her. The speedometer was climbing rapidly. "Slow down," he warned.

"Or what, you'll shoot me? You're going to do that anyway, so go ahead." The overpass to the loop was now visible.

"What are you going to do?" She could hear the fear in his voice, and she fed off of it.

"Unless you toss that gun away, I'm going to ram the car into the concrete wall of the overpass," C. J. replied calmly.

He stared at her before giving a short, harsh laugh. "You're crazy. Slow down. You'll kill us both."

He gazed in horror as the overpass grew steadily closer.

"Toss the gun, Ray. I'm already dead. I've got nothing to lose." The speedometer was sitting on one hundred and five. Ray was alternately grabbing the dashboard and waving the pistol.

"Stop, for god's sake," he begged.

"Pitch the gun!"

"C. J.!"

"Toss the goddamn gun!"

The overpass was drawing rapidly closer, and C. J.'s heart was pounding so hard she could barely breathe. She could feel sweat crawling down her temple. The wall was getting too close. She knew she would never be able to deliberately collide with it, but she had to convince him that she would.

He lunged for the wheel but was pulled up short by his seat belt. C. J. struck him across his face with all her strength. "Toss the gun!" she screamed as the overpass loomed before them.

"All right! Just stop!" He pitched the gun behind him and gripped the suitcase in his lap. C. J. released the accelerator and wiped away the sweat that was stinging her eyes. In one swift, unexpected movement he released his seat belt and threw himself on her. Startled by his sudden movement, her first instinct was to dodge him, but there was no room inside the car to maneuver. He grabbed the wheel. The car was still traveling at a high rate of speed and spun wildly around. She tried to regain control but was hampered by the weight of his body across her arms. The car swerved about sharply and tilted at a sickening angle. For one terrible moment it seemed to hang in midair before it rolled over.

C. J. felt a wave of pain shoot through her legs. Ray screamed as the car continued to roll and compress around them. It seemed to roll forever before it gave one last flip to its side and spun wildly down the road. Crushed beneath the weight of Ray's body, C. J. watched the dull gray of the cement wall coming toward them. She curled herself up as small as possible.

"I love you, Lois," she whispered as the car struck the wall and the death loop once more earned its name.

CHAPTER NINE

Through a fog of pain, C. J. heard Lois screaming her name. She tried to fight her way through the blinding haze that clouded her mind, but Lois's voice faded.

When the voice finally came back, C. J. struggled to get her bearings. The car seemed to be lying on its left side. She took a mental assessment of her body. Something sharp was digging into her left knee. She tried to shift away from the object and was assaulted with a wave of pain so raw she cried out. She realized that if the pain was that bad she must still be alive.

A heavy pressure on her side made her aware that something was lying against her. Her left arm was caught up under her body, and her right arm was trapped beneath the steering wheel. She opened her eyes and raised her head to see what it was and found herself staring into Ray's lifeless eyes. Her stomach churned violently, and she began to scream. All of the anguish and fear of the last several hours tore from her throat as she tried to free her arms to push Ray's body away. When her limbs refused to move she slammed her eyes closed. Someone nearby was calling her name again, but she couldn't stop screaming.

"I found her," Lois's voice yelled as a hand closed softly around her right elbow.

"Lois!"

"I'm here, babe. Hold on."

"Get me out of here! Lois, please help me!"

"I'm right here, C. J. Can you feel my hand?" She squeezed her elbow. "We'll get you out. Hold on a couple more minutes. They're getting the equipment now."

"He's dead. His eyes are still open," C. J. screamed and choked on a fresh wave of tears. "Get me out of here!" she sobbed and struggled to get free. A searing pain tore through her right leg and stopped her thrashing. Lois was talking to her. C. J. fought to focus on Lois's voice.

"It's going to be all right," Lois assured her. "Close your eyes, but keep talking to me."

C. J.'s panic lessened as she listened to Lois's calm voice talking to her. She knew Lois would get her out. C. J. closed her eyes, but the darkness was too much. She opened them again quickly but was careful not to look up at Ray.

"Where are you?" C. J. asked, and tried to see Lois's hand on her elbow, but there was too much debris. "I can't see you." C. J.'s left pant leg felt wet; she tried to wriggle her toes and found they were sticky. She realized she could no longer feel her right leg.

"Someone hand me a flashlight," Lois yelled. C. J. heard a flurry of noise, and then Lois's voice was back. "C. J., can you see the light?"

A bright beam of light appeared to C. J.'s right. She could see a tiny patch of Lois's arm poking through a small opening created when the front end of the car had crunched up against the windshield. The light became her salvation. As she lay watching the light, things didn't seem as frightening as they had earlier. In fact, C. J. was so tired, she could almost fall asleep. She attributed her increasing calmness to Lois's presence.

"C. J., they have the equipment ready. They're going to start cutting. I have to move out of their way, but I'll be right here. Cover your face if you can and close your eyes."

The thought of Lois letting go of her sent a new wave of fear through her.

"Don't leave me!" she screamed as she attempted to wrench her arm free to grasp Lois's hand but couldn't.

"I'll be right out here. I promise you I won't go far." Lois's voice was moving away from her.

C. J. closed her eyes and forced herself not to panic. There was a teeth-grinding screech when the saw bit into metal. As she lay waiting, the calmness descended over her again, only to be disturbed seconds

144

later by lights so bright they burned through her eyelids.

And then Lois was there, smoothing her hair back away from her face. "Oh my god," she heard Lois murmur. A choir of voices began to yell.

"Get her out of there!" Lois shouted.

"Officer Franklin, you'll have to move." A female voice other than Lois's sounded calm, but urgent. Hands were gently touching C. J.

"I'll be right here. I love you," Lois whispered into her ear. She heard Lois's voice urging someone to keep talking to her. C. J. was growing too tired to keep her eyes open.

The calm woman was saying something to her. Irritated, C. J. wanted to tell her to shut up so she could sleep, but she was too tired. The voice continued until C. J. decided she should try to answer her, then maybe she would be quiet. "Ms. Riley, we'll soon have you free," the woman assured her.

C. J. sensed a lot of activity around her. The weight that had been Ray was lifted from her side. She tried to open her eyes, but the lids were too heavy. If they would just all be quiet long enough for her to take a short nap. Lois's voice was still calling to her from a distance, and hands were gently trying to ease her out. She wanted to tell them it was all right to move her because it no longer hurt. A hand pressed against her neck, and a radio crackled near her ear. The calm woman's voice was back explaining that they were going to have to cut the steering wheel away before they could remove her. The screech of the saw began again. C. J. searched the voices around her for Lois's. It was far away, and she tried to reach toward it, but the effort was too great. Somewhere near at hand the woman's voice was no longer calm. C. J. tried to focus.

". . . losing her," was all she heard.

A soft glow appeared, and C. J. let herself drift toward it. Far away she could see the beautiful face she remembered from her childhood. Her mother was smiling. C. J. moved toward her, and the strong, loving arms she remembered were around her again.

"I never got to say good-bye," C. J. whispered. "You left before I could tell you how much I loved you."

Then the voice she had never thought to hear again was murmuring. C. J. strained to hear what her mother was saying.

"I always knew."

"Why did you leave?" C. J. cried into the comforting shoulder.

"It was time," she answered, stroking C. J.'s hair. "You've got to go back now," she whispered. "It's not your time. You still have a lot to do."

C. J. tried to protest, but the smiling face began to fade. Someone was pounding on her chest. She reached for the fading image and screamed for her mother as a jolt of pain shot through her body. She was suddenly gasping for air, and she sensed rather than saw the people around her. Somewhere very close Lois was screaming her name. There was a flurry of activity as she was transferred from the ground to a stretcher. She sought to return to the place she had just left, but Lois kept calling her and pulling her back. She felt the stretcher bump and slide, then Lois's voice was there, her breath on C. J.'s face, her hand caressing her cheek. Something cool and wet hit

C. J.'s cheek. She opened her eyes, thinking that the rain had finally begun. Instead of rain, she found Lois's tear-stained face above hers.

"Why are you crying?" she heard herself asking.

Lois answered by kissing her cheek.

"I saw my mom," she said, and she smiled at the memory.

Lois placed her cheek against C. J.'s. "Rest now," she whispered.

"Will you be here when I wake up?"

Lois raised her head and stared into C. J.'s eyes. "I'll be here for as long as you want me." Her lips brushed lightly across C. J.'s.

EPILOGUE
Exactly One Year Later

C. J. stood in her robe in front of a large bay window and watched the sun slowly sink beyond a wide field of bluebonnets. She made a mental note to call James and remind him to bring his camera with him tomorrow. He and Ron were coming up for the weekend. Ron had finally confessed his unhappiness to James, and they were working hard to rebuild their relationship. C. J. heard the sound of the back door closing and knew Lois had finished feeding the horses. She turned her attention back to the view before her. There was still so much they wanted to do.

The sound of the shower running reached her. She looked around with a sense of contentment. They had purchased this house and sixty acres nine months ago. It was located deep in the Hill Country, away from the noise and stress of the city. C. J. leaned over and flipped a lamp on. She still had some problems with darkness. She limped slightly as she made her way to the sofa and sat down.

She had been confined to a wheelchair for three months after the accident. In addition to massive internal injuries, both of her legs had been broken and her right knee crushed. After four operations and months of physical therapy, she was able to walk with only a slight limp.

During the past year, life had taken on a new meaning for her and Lois. For now, the most important thing for them was that they were together. They had come too close to losing each other.

Captain Avery, the officer who had wanted to refuse the ransom payment, had promptly started an investigation on Lois, using the state's sodomy law as grounds to try to dismiss her. He had no evidence against her other than her behavior of that night. Several other officers testified on Lois's behalf, and the charges were eventually dropped due to lack of evidence. Days after the charges were dropped, Lois finally confessed to C. J. that the job no longer held the same appeal it had when she was a young rookie. She told C. J. of her dream of someday retiring from the police department and raising quarter horses.

Several weeks later, C. J. managed to convince her to leave the department. They borrowed money from C. J.'s father for the down payment for the ranch. He had tried to give it to them, but C. J. was adamant. This was going to be hers and Lois's. They would work outside jobs until they could make the ranch pay for itself. C. J. found a job as a cashier at a feed store, and Lois worked as a security guard for the local bank. Money was always tight, but as hokey as it sounded they had each other.

Riley Produce seemed to be more stable. C. J. shuddered, thinking about what would have happened to the business had Ray managed to escape with the ransom money. The cash had been safety returned as soon as the investigation had been completed.

Her father admitted how much he had hated being away from his work, but did agree to slow down and pace himself. He now only worked four days a week.

Mary Acosta took on a large part of the workload and the rest was passed on to others. C. J. knew that someday when he decided to retire, she would again be faced with deciding how Riley Produce would fit into her life, but that was in the future and she was living for today.

Lois interrupted her musing. "You ran off and left me in the barn," she accused, as she toweled her hair dry.

"I wanted to make sure I had everything ready when you came in," C. J. said with a sly smile.

Lois shook back her short black hair and tossed the towel onto the stone fireplace mantel. "You'd have what ready?"

C. J. reached beneath the coffee table and brought out an ice bucket containing a bottle of ginger ale and two glasses. Champagne would have been nice, but it no longer fit into their budget.

"What's this for?" Lois smiled and sat next to her on the sofa.

C. J. remained silent as she opened the bottle and poured them each a glass. She handed one to Lois and lifted her own in a toast. "To life and love."

Lois gently touched her glass to C. J.'s and sipped. They sat in comfortable silence. They rarely spoke of that night. It was still too painful.

"I love you," Lois said as she reached for her.

C. J. stared boldly into her eyes and drew closer. Their lips met, softly searching. C. J. caught her breath as her stomach did a now familiar series of somersaults. She let her lips slide down Lois's throat and linger in the small hollow of her neck. Lois moaned and pulled away long enough to take their glasses and place them on the table. As she turned around, C. J. pushed her back onto the sofa and untied the belt to Lois's robe. She ran her tongue across a firm nipple and smiled to herself when Lois groaned. She kissed her and pulled Lois's bottom lip between her teeth, sucking it in.

Lois's tongue probed demandingly as she arched her body upward against C. J.'s. Grabbing Lois's hips, she pulled her closer. Her hand glided along soft curves until they each held a full, swelling breast. She lowered her head to a hard rosy nipple and traced the surface with the tip of her tongue until Lois was moaning. C. J. slid slowly to the other breast and flicked her tongue gently across it before inching her way down Lois's arching body. Her lips brushed the thick, curly, black patch, and she tongued her way into the rich moisture. The sofa was too short. C. J. pulled

Lois upright and kissed her deeply as her own robe was thrown to the floor. C. J. swung Lois's feet off the sofa and knelt between her long smooth legs. She kneaded her breasts as their tongues entwined. C. J. again trailed her tongue down the well-muscled stomach and immersed it into the sweet damp moisture. She sucked the swollen bud into her mouth, sliding her fingers deep inside until Lois moaned and grabbed C. J.'s head, pulling her closer. C. J. felt herself being drawn to the edge as Lois's body shuddered and the hands on her head became viselike in their grasp. After the grip relaxed, she crawled onto the sofa beside Lois and held her until her breathing calmed. Lois began kissing her.

"Before we get too involved, let's go to bed," C. J. suggested, pulling Lois up. "This sofa is entirely too short."

"I'm not sure I can wait that long," Lois murmured into her ear.

C. J.'s legs turned to butter as Lois's tongue deftly slipped into her ear. Locked in a fierce kiss, they stumbled toward the bedroom. They made it as far as the hallway before C. J. found her shoulders pinned to the wall and Lois's insisting hand pushing between her legs. "I can't stand up," C. J. protested.

"Let me hold you." Lois's free arm curled around C. J. and pulled her against her. The other hand worked a steady rhythm back and forth between C. J.'s legs. With an agonizing slowness, a finger pushed inside, a second finger slid in on the next stroke, and finally a third filled her. Lois's hand moved faster until C. J.'s knees refused to hold her any longer. Lois held her upright and continued her gentle onslaught until C. J. screamed out and gripped

Lois's body to hers. Lois's fingers slowed as she eased C. J. to the carpet.

"Don't stop," C. J. begged as Lois slid her body alongside her.

"I'll never stop," Lois promised, her mouth capturing C. J.'s.

LOOKING FOR NAIAD?

Buy our books at
www.naiadpress.com

or call our toll-free number
1-800-533-1973

or by fax (24 hours a day)
1-850-539-9731

A few of the publications of
THE NAIAD PRESS, INC.
P.O. Box 10543   Tallahassee, Florida 32302
Phone (850) 539-5965
Toll-Free Order Number: 1-800-533-1973
Web Site: WWW.NAIADPRESS.COM
Mail orders welcome. Please include 15% postage.
Write or call for our free catalog which also features an
incredible selection of lesbian videos.

ONE OF OUR OWN by Diane Salvatore. 240 pp. Carly Matson
has a secret. So does Lela Johns.   ISBN 1-56280-243-7 $11.95

DOUBLE TAKEOUT by Tracey Richardson. 176 pp. 3rd Stevie
Houston mystery.   ISBN 1-56280-244-5   11.95

CAPTIVE HEART by Frankie J. Jones. 176 pp. Love in the
fast lane or heartside romance?   ISBN 1-56280-258-5   11.95

WICKED GOOD TIME by Diana Tremain Braund. 224 pp. In
charge at work, out of control in her heart. ISBN 1-56280-241-0   11.95

SNAKE EYES by Pat Welch. 256 pp. 7th Helen Black mystery.
                                              ISBN 1-56280-242-9   11.95

CHANGE OF HEART by Linda Hill. 176 pp. High fashion and
love in a glamorous world.   ISBN 1-56280-238-0   11.95

UNSTRUNG HEART by Robbi Sommers. 176 pp. Putting life
in order again.   ISBN 1-56280-239-9   11.95

BIRDS OF A FEATHER by Jackie Calhoun. 240 pp. Life begins
with love.   ISBN 1-56280-240-2   11.95

THE DRIVE by Trisha Todd. 176 pp. The star of *Claire of the*
Moon tells all!   ISBN 1-56280-237-2   11.95

BOTH SIDES by Saxon Bennett. 240 pp. A community of
women falling in and out of love.   ISBN 1-56280-236-4   11.95

WATERMARK by Karin Kallmaker. 256 pp. One burning
question . . . how to lead her back to love? ISBN 1-56280-235-6   11.95

THE OTHER WOMAN by Ann O'Leary. 240 pp. Her roguish
way draws women like a magnet.   ISBN 1-56280-234-8   11.95

SILVER THREADS by Lyn Denison.208 pp. Finding her way
back to love . . .   ISBN 1-56280-231-3   11.95

CHIMNEY ROCK BLUES by Janet McClellan. 224 pp. 4th Tru
North mystery.   ISBN 1-56280-233-X   11.95

OMAHA'S BELL by Penny Hayes. 208 pp. Orphaned Keeley
Delaney woos the lovely Prudence Morris.　　ISBN 1-56280-232-1　　11.95

SIXTH SENSE by Kate Calloway. 224 pp. 6th Cassidy James
mystery.　　ISBN 1-56280-228-3　　11.95

DAWN OF THE DANCE by Marianne K. Martin. 224 pp. A dance
with an old friend, nothing more . . . yeah!　　ISBN 1-56280-229-1　　11.95

WEDDING BELL BLUES by Julia Watts. 240 pp. Love, family,
and a recipe for success.　　ISBN 1-56280-230-5　　11.95

THOSE WHO WAIT by Peggy J. Herring. 160 pp. Two
sisters . . . in love with the same woman.　　ISBN 1-56280-223-2　　11.95

WHISPERS IN THE WIND by Frankie J. Jones. 192 pp. "If you
don't want this," she whispered, "all you have to say is 'stop.' "
　　ISBN 1-56280-226-7　　11.95

WHEN SOME BODY DISAPPEARS by Therese Szymanski.
192 pp. 3rd Brett Higgins mystery.　　ISBN 1-56280-227-5　　11.95

THE WAY LIFE SHOULD BE by Diana Braund. 240 pp. Which
one will teach her the true meaning of love?　　ISBN 1-56280-221-6　　11.95

UNTIL THE END by Kaye Davis. 256pp. 3rd Maris Middleton
mystery.　　ISBN 1-56280-222-4　　11.95

FIFTH WHEEL by Kate Calloway. 224 pp. 5th Cassidy James
mystery.　　ISBN 1-56280-218-6　　11.95

JUST YESTERDAY by Linda Hill. 176 pp. Reliving all the
passion of yesterday.　　ISBN 1-56280-219-4　　11.95

THE TOUCH OF YOUR HAND edited by Barbara Grier and
Christine Cassidy. 304 pp. Erotic love stories by Naiad Press
authors.　　ISBN 1-56280-220-8　　14.95

WINDROW GARDEN by Janet McClellan. 192 pp. They discover
a passion they never dreamed possible.　　ISBN 1-56280-216-X　　11.95

PAST DUE by Claire McNab. 224 pp. 10th Carol Ashton
mystery.　　ISBN 1-56280-217-8　　11.95

CHRISTABEL by Laura Adams. 224 pp. Two captive hearts and
the passion that will set them free.　　ISBN 1-56280-214-3　　11.95

PRIVATE PASSIONS by Laura DeHart Young. 192 pp. An
unforgettable new portrait of lesbian love . . .　　ISBN 1-56280-215-1　　11.95

BAD MOON RISING by Barbara Johnson. 208 pp. 2nd Colleen
Fitzgerald mystery.　　ISBN 1-56280-211-9　　11.95

RIVER QUAY by Janet McClellan. 208 pp. 3rd Tru North
mystery.　　ISBN 1-56280-212-7　　11.95

ENDLESS LOVE by Lisa Shapiro. 272 pp. To believe, once
again, that love can be forever.　　ISBN 1-56280-213-5　　11.95

FALLEN FROM GRACE by Pat Welch. 256 pp. 6th Helen Black
mystery.　　ISBN 1-56280-209-7　　11.95

THE NAKED EYE by Catherine Ennis. 208 pp. Her lover in the camera's eye . . . ISBN 1-56280-210-0   11.95

OVER THE LINE by Tracey Richardson. 176 pp. 2nd Stevie Houston mystery. ISBN 1-56280-202-X   11.95

JULIA'S SONG by Ann O'Leary. 208 pp. Strangely disturbing . . . strangely exciting. ISBN 1-56280-197-X   11.95

LOVE IN THE BALANCE by Marianne K. Martin. 256 pp. Weighing the costs of love . . . ISBN 1-56280-199-6   11.95

PIECE OF MY HEART by Julia Watts. 208 pp. All the stuff that dreams are made of — ISBN 1-56280-206-2   11.95

MAKING UP FOR LOST TIME by Karin Kallmaker. 240 pp. Nobody does it better . . . ISBN 1-56280-196-1   11.95

GOLD FEVER by Lyn Denison. 224 pp. By author of *Dream Lover.* ISBN 1-56280-201-1   11.95

WHEN THE DEAD SPEAK by Therese Szymanski. 224 pp. 2nd Brett Higgins mystery. ISBN 1-56280-198-8   11.95

FOURTH DOWN by Kate Calloway. 240 pp. 4th Cassidy James mystery. ISBN 1-56280-205-4   11.95

A MOMENT'S INDISCRETION by Peggy J. Herring. 176 pp. There's a fine line between love and lust . . . ISBN 1-56280-194-5   11.95

CITY LIGHTS/COUNTRY CANDLES by Penny Hayes. 208 pp. About the women she has known . . . ISBN 1-56280-195-3   11.95

POSSESSIONS by Kaye Davis. 240 pp. 2nd Maris Middleton mystery. ISBN 1-56280-192-9   11.95

A QUESTION OF LOVE by Saxon Bennett. 208 pp. Every woman is granted one great love. ISBN 1-56280-205-4   11.95

RHYTHM TIDE by Frankie J. Jones. 160 pp. . . . to desire passionately and be passionately desired. ISBN 1-56280-189-9   11.95

PENN VALLEY PHOENIX by Janet McClellan. 208 pp. 2nd Tru North Mystery. ISBN 1-56280-200-3   11.95

BY RESERVATION ONLY by Jackie Calhoun. 240 pp. A chance for true happiness. ISBN 1-56280-191-0   11.95

OLD BLACK MAGIC by Jaye Maiman. 272 pp. 9th Robin Miller mystery. ISBN 1-56280-175-9   11.95

LEGACY OF LOVE by Marianne K. Martin. 240 pp. Women will do anything for her . . . ISBN 1-56280-184-8   11.95

LETTING GO by Ann O'Leary. 160 pp. Laura, at 39, in love with 23-year-old Kate. ISBN 1-56280-183-X   11.95

LADY BE GOOD edited by Barbara Grier and Christine Cassidy. 288 pp. Erotic stories by Naiad Press authors. ISBN 1-56280-180-5   14.95

CHAIN LETTER by Claire McNab. 288 pp. 9th Carol Ashton mystery. ISBN 1-56280-181-3   11.95

NIGHT VISION by Laura Adams. 256 pp. Erotic fantasy romance
by "famous" author.   ISBN 1-56280-182-1   11.95

SEA TO SHINING SEA by Lisa Shapiro. 256 pp. Unable to resist
the raging passion . . .   ISBN 1-56280-177-5   11.95

THIRD DEGREE by Kate Calloway. 224 pp. 3rd Cassidy James
mystery.   ISBN 1-56280-185-6   11.95

WHEN THE DANCING STOPS by Therese Szymanski. 272 pp.
1st Brett Higgins mystery.   ISBN 1-56280-186-4   11.95

PHASES OF THE MOON by Julia Watts. 192 pp. . . . . hungry
for everything life has to offer.   ISBN 1-56280-176-7   11.95

BABY IT'S COLD by Jaye Maiman. 256 pp. 5th Robin Miller
mystery.   ISBN 1-56280-156-2   10.95

CLASS REUNION by Linda Hill. 176 pp. The girl from her
past . . .   ISBN 1-56280-178-3   11.95

DREAM LOVER by Lyn Denison. 224 pp. A soft, sensuous,
romantic fantasy.   ISBN 1-56280-173-1   11.95

FORTY LOVE by Diana Simmonds. 288 pp. Joyous, heart-
warming romance.   ISBN 1-56280-171-6   11.95

IN THE MOOD by Robbi Sommers. 160 pp. The queen of
erotic tension!   ISBN 1-56280-172-4   11.95

SWIMMING CAT COVE by Lauren Douglas. 192 pp. 2nd
Allison O'Neil Mystery.   ISBN 1-56280-168-6   11.95

THE LOVING LESBIAN by Claire McNab and Sharon Gedan.
240 pp. Explore the experiences that make lesbian love unique.
                                       ISBN 1-56280-169-4   14.95

COURTED by Celia Cohen. 160 pp. Sparkling romantic
encounter.   ISBN 1-56280-166-X   11.95

SEASONS OF THE HEART by Jackie Calhoun. 240 pp. Romance
through the years.   ISBN 1-56280-167-8   11.95

K. C. BOMBER by Janet McClellan. 208 pp. 1st Tru North
mystery.   ISBN 1-56280-157-0   11.95

LAST RITES by Tracey Richardson. 192 pp. 1st Stevie Houston
mystery.   ISBN 1-56280-164-3   11.95

EMBRACE IN MOTION by Karin Kallmaker. 256 pp. A whirlwind
love affair.   ISBN 1-56280-165-1   11.95

HOT CHECK by Peggy J. Herring. 192 pp. Will workaholic Alice
fall for guitarist Ricky?   ISBN 1-56280-163-5   11.95

OLD TIES by Saxon Bennett. 176 pp. Can Cleo surrender to a
passionate new love?   ISBN 1-56280-159-7   11.95

LOVE ON THE LINE by Laura DeHart Young. 176 pp. Will Stef
win Kay's heart?   ISBN 1-56280-162-7   11.95

DEVIL'S LEG CROSSING by Kaye Davis. 192 pp. 1st Maris
Middleton mystery.   ISBN 1-56280-158-9   11.95

COSTA BRAVA by Marta Balletbo Coll. 144 pp. Read the book,
see the movie!   ISBN 1-56280-153-8   11.95

MEETING MAGDALENE & OTHER STORIES by
Marilyn Freeman. 144 pp. Read the book, see the movie!
                                            ISBN 1-56280-170-8   11.95

SECOND FIDDLE by Kate 208 pp. 2nd P.I. Cassidy James
mystery.   ISBN 1-56280-169-6   11.95

LAUREL by Isabel Miller. 128 pp. By the author of the beloved
Patience and Sarah.   ISBN 1-56280-146-5   10.95

LOVE OR MONEY by Jackie Calhoun. 240 pp. The romance of
real life.   ISBN 1-56280-147-3   10.95

SMOKE AND MIRRORS by Pat Welch. 224 pp. 5th Helen Black
Mystery.   ISBN 1-56280-143-0   10.95

DANCING IN THE DARK edited by Barbara Grier & Christine
Cassidy. 272 pp. Erotic love stories by Naiad Press authors.
                                            ISBN 1-56280-144-9   14.95

TIME AND TIME AGAIN by Catherine Ennis. 176 pp. Passionate
love affair.   ISBN 1-56280-145-7   10.95

PAXTON COURT by Diane Salvatore. 256 pp. Erotic and wickedly
funny contemporary tale about the business of learning to live
together.   ISBN 1-56280-114-7   10.95

INNER CIRCLE by Claire McNab. 208 pp. 8th Carol Ashton
Mystery.   ISBN 1-56280-135-X   11.95

LESBIAN SEX: AN ORAL HISTORY by Susan Johnson.
240 pp. Need we say more?   ISBN 1-56280-142-2   14.95

WILD THINGS by Karin Kallmaker. 240 pp. By the undisputed
mistress of lesbian romance.   ISBN 1-56280-139-2   11.95

THE GIRL NEXT DOOR by Mindy Kaplan. 208 pp. Just what
you d expect.   ISBN 1-56280-140-6   11.95

NOW AND THEN by Penny Hayes. 240 pp. Romance on the
westward journey.   ISBN 1-56280-121-X   11.95

HEART ON FIRE by Diana Simmonds. 176 pp. The romantic and
erotic rival of *Curious Wine.*   ISBN 1-56280-152-X   11.95

DEATH AT LAVENDER BAY by Lauren Wright Douglas. 208 pp.
1st Allison O'Neil Mystery.   ISBN 1-56280-085-X   11.95

YES I SAID YES I WILL by Judith McDaniel. 272 pp. Hot
romance by famous author.   ISBN 1-56280-138-4   11.95

FORBIDDEN FIRES by Margaret C. Anderson. Edited by Mathilda
Hills. 176 pp. Famous author's "unpublished" Lesbian romance.
                                            ISBN 1-56280-123-6   21.95

SIDE TRACKS by Teresa Stores. 160 pp. Gender-bending
Lesbians on the road. ISBN 1-56280-122-8 10.95

WILDWOOD FLOWERS by Julia Watts. 208 pp. Hilarious and
heart-warming tale of true love. ISBN 1-56280-127-9 10.95

NEVER SAY NEVER by Linda Hill. 224 pp. Rule #1: Never get
involved with . . . ISBN 1-56280-126-0 11.95

THE WISH LIST by Saxon Bennett. 192 pp. Romance through
the years. ISBN 1-56280-125-2 10.95

OUT OF THE NIGHT by Kris Bruyer. 192 pp. Spine-tingling
thriller. ISBN 1-56280-120-1 10.95

LOVE'S HARVEST by Peggy J. Herring. 176 pp. by the author of
Once More With Feeling. ISBN 1-56280-117-1 10.95

FAMILY SECRETS by Laura DeHart Young. 208 pp. Enthralling
romance and suspense. ISBN 1-56280-119-8 10.95

INLAND PASSAGE by Jane Rule. 288 pp. Tales exploring conven-
tional & unconventional relationships. ISBN 0-930044-56-8 10.95

DOUBLE BLUFF by Claire McNab. 208 pp. 7th Carol Ashton
Mystery. ISBN 1-56280-096-5 10.95

BAR GIRLS by Lauran Hoffman. 176 pp. See the movie, read
the book! ISBN 1-56280-115-5 10.95

THE FIRST TIME EVER edited by Barbara Grier & Christine
Cassidy. 272 pp. Love stories by Naiad Press authors.
ISBN 1-56280-086-8 14.95

MISS PETTIBONE AND MISS McGRAW by Brenda Weathers.
208 pp. A charming ghostly love story. ISBN 1-56280-151-1 10.95

CHANGES by Jackie Calhoun. 208 pp. Involved romance and
relationships. ISBN 1-56280-083-3 10.95

FAIR PLAY by Rose Beecham. 256 pp. An Amanda Valentine
Mystery. ISBN 1-56280-081-7 10.95

PAYBACK by Celia Cohen. 176 pp. A gripping thriller of romance,
revenge and betrayal. ISBN 1-56280-084-1 10.95

THE BEACH AFFAIR by Barbara Johnson. 224 pp. Sizzling
summer romance/mystery/intrigue. ISBN 1-56280-090-6 10.95

GETTING THERE by Robbi Sommers. 192 pp. Nobody does it
like Robbi! ISBN 1-56280-099-X 10.95

FINAL CUT by Lisa Haddock. 208 pp. 2nd Carmen Ramirez
Mystery. ISBN 1-56280-088-4 10.95

FLASHPOINT by Katherine V. Forrest. 256 pp. A Lesbian
blockbuster! ISBN 1-56280-079-5 10.95

CLAIRE OF THE MOON by Nicole Conn. Audio Book —
Read by Marianne Hyatt. ISBN 1-56280-113-9 16.95

FOR LOVE AND FOR LIFE: INTIMATE PORTRAITS OF
LESBIAN COUPLES by Susan Johnson. 224 pp.
ISBN 1-56280-091-4   14.95

DEVOTION by Mindy Kaplan. 192 pp. See the movie — read
the book!   ISBN 1-56280-093-0   10.95

SOMEONE TO WATCH by Jaye Maiman. 272 pp. 4th Robin
Miller Mystery.   ISBN 1-56280-095-7   10.95

GREENER THAN GRASS by Jennifer Fulton. 208 pp. A young
woman — a stranger in her bed.   ISBN 1-56280-092-2   10.95

TRAVELS WITH DIANA HUNTER by Regine Sands. Erotic
lesbian romp. Audio Book (2 cassettes)   ISBN 1-56280-107-4   16.95

CABIN FEVER by Carol Schmidt. 256 pp. Sizzling suspense
and passion.   ISBN 1-56280-089-1   10.95

THERE WILL BE NO GOODBYES by Laura DeHart Young. 192
pp. Romantic love, strength, and friendship.   ISBN 1-56280-103-1   10.95

FAULTLINE by Sheila Ortiz Taylor. 144 pp. Joyous comic
lesbian novel.   ISBN 1-56280-108-2   9.95

OPEN HOUSE by Pat Welch. 176 pp. 4th Helen Black Mystery.
ISBN 1-56280-102-3   10.95

ONCE MORE WITH FEELING by Peggy J. Herring. 240 pp.
Lighthearted, loving romantic adventure.   ISBN 1-56280-089-2   11.95

WHISPERS by Kris Bruyer. 176 pp. Romantic ghost story.
ISBN 1-56280-082-5   10.95

NIGHT SONGS by Penny Mickelbury. 224 pp. 2nd Gianna
Maglione Mystery.   ISBN 1-56280-097-3   10.95

GETTING TO THE POINT by Teresa Stores. 256 pp. Classic
southern Lesbian novel.   ISBN 1-56280-100-7   10.95

PAINTED MOON by Karin Kallmaker. 224 pp. Delicious
Kallmaker romance.   ISBN 1-56280-075-2   11.95

THE MYSTERIOUS NAIAD edited by Katherine V. Forrest &
Barbara Grier. 320 pp. Love stories by Naiad Press authors.
ISBN 1-56280-074-4   14.95

DAUGHTERS OF A CORAL DAWN by Katherine V. Forrest.
240 pp. Tenth Anniversay Edition.   ISBN 1-56280-104-X   11.95

BODY GUARD by Claire McNab. 208 pp. 6th Carol Ashton
Mystery.   ISBN 1-56280-073-6   11.95

CACTUS LOVE by Lee Lynch. 192 pp. Stories by the beloved
storyteller.   ISBN 1-56280-071-X   9.95

SECOND GUESS by Rose Beecham. 216 pp. An Amanda
Valentine Mystery.   ISBN 1-56280-069-8   9.95

A RAGE OF MAIDENS by Lauren Wright Douglas. 240 pp.
6th Caitlin Reece Mystery.   ISBN 1-56280-068-X   10.95

THE SPY IN QUESTION by Amanda Kyle Williams. 256 pp.
A Madison McGuire Mystery. ISBN 1-56280-037-X 9.95

SAVING GRACE by Jennifer Fulton. 240 pp. Adventure and
romantic entanglement. ISBN 1-56280-051-5 11.95

CURIOUS WINE by Katherine V. Forrest. 176 pp. Tenth Anniver-
sary Edition. The most popular contemporary Lesbian love story.
ISBN 1-56280-053-1 11.95
Audio Book (2 cassettes) ISBN 1-56280-105-8 16.95

CHAUTAUQUA by Catherine Ennis. 192 pp. Exciting, romantic
adventure. ISBN 1-56280-032-9 9.95

A PROPER BURIAL by Pat Welch. 192 pp. 3rd Helen Black
Mystery. ISBN 1-56280-033-7 9.95

SILVERLAKE HEAT: A Novel of Suspense by Carol Schmidt.
240 pp. Rhonda is as hot as Laney's dreams. ISBN 1-56280-031-0 9.95

LOVE, ZENA BETH by Diane Salvatore. 224 pp. The most talked
about lesbian novel of the nineties! ISBN 1-56280-030-2 10.95

A DOORYARD FULL OF FLOWERS by Isabel Miller. 160 pp.
Stories incl. 2 sequels to *Patience and Sarah.* ISBN 1-56280-029-9 9.95

MURDER BY TRADITION by Katherine V. Forrest. 288 pp. 4th
Kate Delafield Mystery. ISBN 1-56280-002-7 11.95

THE EROTIC NAIAD edited by Katherine V. Forrest & Barbara
Grier. 224 pp. Love stories by Naiad Press authors.
ISBN 1-56280-026-4 14.95

DEAD CERTAIN by Claire McNab. 224 pp. 5th Carol Ashton
Mystery. ISBN 1-56280-027-2 9.95

CRAZY FOR LOVING by Jaye Maiman. 320 pp. 2nd Robin Miller
Mystery. ISBN 1-56280-025-6 11.95

UNCERTAIN COMPANIONS by Robbi Sommers. 204 pp.
Steamy, erotic novel. ISBN 1-56280-017-5 11.95

A TIGER'S HEART by Lauren W. Douglas. 240 pp. 4th Caitlin
Reece Mystery. ISBN 1-56280-018-3 9.95

PAPERBACK ROMANCE by Karin Kallmaker. 256 pp. A
delicious romance. ISBN 1-56280-019-1 10.95

THE LAVENDER HOUSE MURDER by Nikki Baker. 224 pp.
2nd Virginia Kelly Mystery. ISBN 1-56280-012-4 9.95

PASSION BAY by Jennifer Fulton. 224 pp. Passionate romance,
virgin beaches, tropical skies. ISBN 1-56280-028-0 10.95

STICKS AND STONES by Jackie Calhoun. 208 pp. Contemporary
lesbian lives and loves. ISBN 1-56280-020-5 9.95
Audio Book (2 cassettes) ISBN 1-56280-106-6 16.95

UNDER THE SOUTHERN CROSS by Claire McNab. 192 pp.
Romantic nights Down Under. ISBN 1-56280-011-6 11.95

GRASSY FLATS by Penny Hayes. 256 pp. Lesbian romance in the '30s. ISBN 1-56280-010-8   9.95

THE END OF APRIL by Penny Sumner. 240 pp. 1st Victoria Cross Mystery. ISBN 1-56280-007-8   8.95

KISS AND TELL by Robbi Sommers. 192 pp. Scorching stories by the author of *Pleasures.* ISBN 1-56280-005-1   11.95

STILL WATERS by Pat Welch. 208 pp. 2nd Helen Black Mystery. ISBN 0-941483-97-5   9.95

TO LOVE AGAIN by Evelyn Kennedy. 208 pp. Wildly romantic love story. ISBN 0-941483-85-1   11.95

IN THE GAME by Nikki Baker. 192 pp. 1st Virginia Kelly Mystery. ISBN 1-56280-004-3   9.95

STRANDED by Camarin Grae. 320 pp. Entertaining, riveting adventure. ISBN 0-941483-99-1   9.95

THE DAUGHTERS OF ARTEMIS by Lauren Wright Douglas. 240 pp. 3rd Caitlin Reece Mystery. ISBN 0-941483-95-9   9.95

CLEARWATER by Catherine Ennis. 176 pp. Romantic secrets of a small Louisiana town. ISBN 0-941483-65-7   8.95

THE HALLELUJAH MURDERS by Dorothy Tell. 176 pp. 2nd Poppy Dillworth Mystery. ISBN 0-941483-88-6   8.95

BENEDICTION by Diane Salvatore. 272 pp. Striking, contemporary romantic novel. ISBN 0-941483-90-8   11.95

COP OUT by Claire McNab. 208 pp. 4th Carol Ashton Mystery. ISBN 0-941483-84-3   10.95

THE BEVERLY MALIBU by Katherine V. Forrest. 288 pp. 3rd Kate Delafield Mystery. ISBN 0-941483-48-7   11.95

THE PROVIDENCE FILE by Amanda Kyle Williams. 256 pp. A Madison McGuire Mystery. ISBN 0-941483-92-4   8.95

I LEFT MY HEART by Jaye Maiman. 320 pp. 1st Robin Miller Mystery. ISBN 0-941483-72-X   11.95

THE PRICE OF SALT by Patricia Highsmith (writing as Claire Morgan). 288 pp. Classic lesbian novel, first issued in 1952 . . . acknowledged by its author under her own, very famous, name. ISBN 1-56280-003-5   11.95

SIDE BY SIDE by Isabel Miller. 256 pp. From beloved author of *Patience and Sarah.* ISBN 0-941483-77-0   10.95

STAYING POWER: LONG TERM LESBIAN COUPLES by Susan E. Johnson. 352 pp. Joys of coupledom. ISBN 0-941-483-75-4   14.95

SLICK by Camarin Grae. 304 pp. Exotic, erotic adventure. ISBN 0-941483-74-6   9.95

NINTH LIFE by Lauren Wright Douglas. 256 pp. 2nd Caitlin Reece Mystery. ISBN 0-941483-50-9   9.95

PLAYERS by Robbi Sommers. 192 pp. Sizzling, erotic novel.
ISBN 0-941483-73-8   9.95

MURDER AT RED ROOK RANCH by Dorothy Tell. 224 pp.
1st Poppy Dillworth Mystery.   ISBN 0-941483-80-0   8.95

A ROOM FULL OF WOMEN by Elisabeth Nonas. 256 pp.
Contemporary Lesbian lives.   ISBN 0-941483-69-X   9.95

THEME FOR DIVERSE INSTRUMENTS by Jane Rule. 208 pp.
Powerful romantic lesbian stories.   ISBN 0-941483-63-0   8.95

CLUB 12 by Amanda Kyle Williams. 288 pp. Espionage thriller
featuring a lesbian agent!   ISBN 0-941483-64-9   9.95

DEATH DOWN UNDER by Claire McNab. 240 pp. 3rd Carol
Ashton Mystery.   ISBN 0-941483-39-8   11.95

MONTANA FEATHERS by Penny Hayes. 256 pp. Vivian and
Elizabeth find love in frontier Montana. ISBN 0-941483-61-4 9.95

THERE'S SOMETHING I'VE BEEN MEANING TO TELL YOU
Ed. by Loralee MacPike. 288 pp. Gay men and lesbians coming out
to their children.   ISBN 0-941483-44-4   9.95

LIFTING BELLY by Gertrude Stein. Ed. by Rebecca Mark. 104 pp.
Erotic poetry.   ISBN 0-941483-51-7   10.95

AFTER THE FIRE by Jane Rule. 256 pp. Warm, human novel by
this incomparable author.   ISBN 0-941483-45-2   8.95

PLEASURES by Robbi Sommers. 204 pp. Unprecedented
eroticism.   ISBN 0-941483-49-5   11.95

EDGEWISE by Camarin Grae. 372 pp. Spellbinding
adventure.   ISBN 0-941483-19-3   9.95

FATAL REUNION by Claire McNab. 224 pp. 2nd Carol Ashton
Mystery.   ISBN 0-941483-40-1   11.95

IN EVERY PORT by Karin Kallmaker. 228 pp. Jessica's sexy,
adventuresome travels.   ISBN 0-941483-37-7   11.95

OF LOVE AND GLORY by Evelyn Kennedy. 192 pp. Exciting
WWII romance.   ISBN 0-941483-32-0   10.95

CLICKING STONES by Nancy Tyler Glenn. 288 pp. Love
transcending time.   ISBN 0-941483-31-2   9.95

SOUTH OF THE LINE by Catherine Ennis. 216 pp. Civil War
adventure.   ISBN 0-941483-29-0   8.95

WOMAN PLUS WOMAN by Dolores Klaich. 300 pp. Supurb
Lesbian overview.   ISBN 0-941483-28-2   9.95

THE FINER GRAIN by Denise Ohio. 216 pp. Brilliant young
college lesbian novel.   ISBN 0-941483-11-8   8.95

LESSONS IN MURDER by Claire McNab. 216 pp. 1st Carol Ashton
Mystery.   ISBN 0-941483-14-2   11.95

YELLOWTHROAT by Penny Hayes. 240 pp. Margarita, bandit, kidnaps Julia. ISBN 0-941483-10-X 8.95

SAPPHISTRY: THE BOOK OF LESBIAN SEXUALITY by Pat Califia. 3d edition, revised. 208 pp. ISBN 0-941483-24-X 12.95

CHERISHED LOVE by Evelyn Kennedy. 192 pp. Erotic Lesbian love story. ISBN 0-941483-08-8 11.95

THE SECRET IN THE BIRD by Camarin Grae. 312 pp. Striking, psychological suspense novel. ISBN 0-941483-05-3 8.95

TO THE LIGHTNING by Catherine Ennis. 208 pp. Romantic Lesbian `Robinson Crusoe adventure. ISBN 0-941483-06-1 8.95

DREAMS AND SWORDS by Katherine V. Forrest. 192 pp. Romantic, erotic, imaginative stories. ISBN 0-941483-03-7 11.95

MEMORY BOARD by Jane Rule. 336 pp. Memorable novel about an aging Lesbian couple. ISBN 0-941483-02-9 12.95

THE ALWAYS ANONYMOUS BEAST by Lauren Wright Douglas. 224 pp. 1st Caitlin Reece Mystery. ISBN 0-941483-04-5 8.95

MURDER AT THE NIGHTWOOD BAR by Katherine V. Forrest. 240 pp. 2nd Kate Delafield Mystery. ISBN 0-930044-92-4 11.95

WINGED DANCER by Camarin Grae. 228 pp. Erotic Lesbian adventure story. ISBN 0-930044-88-6 8.95

PAZ by Camarin Grae. 336 pp. Romantic Lesbian adventurer with the power to change the world. ISBN 0-930044-89-4 8.95

SOUL SNATCHER by Camarin Grae. 224 pp. A puzzle, an adventure, a mystery — Lesbian romance. ISBN 0-930044-90-8 8.95

THE LOVE OF GOOD WOMEN by Isabel Miller. 224 pp. Long-awaited new novel by the author of the beloved *Patience and Sarah.* ISBN 0-930044-81-9 8.95

THE LONG TRAIL by Penny Hayes. 248 pp. Vivid adventures of two women in love in the old west. ISBN 0-930044-76-2 8.95

AN EMERGENCE OF GREEN by Katherine V. Forrest. 288 pp. Powerful novel of sexual discovery. ISBN 0-930044-69-X 11.95

DESERT OF THE HEART by Jane Rule. 224 pp. A classic; basis for the movie *Desert Hearts.* ISBN 0-930044-73-8 12.95

SEX VARIANT WOMEN IN LITERATURE by Jeannette Howard Foster. 448 pp. Literary history. ISBN 0-930044-65-7 8.95

These are just a few of the many Naiad Press titles — we are the oldest and largest lesbian/feminist publishing company in the world. We also offer an enormous selection of lesbian video products. Please request a complete catalog. We offer personal service; we encourage and welcome direct mail orders from individuals who have limited access to bookstores carrying our publications.